ValHamster

BY ANGELA MISRI

DCB

We acknowledge financial support for our publishing activities: the Government
of Canada, through the Canada Book Fund and The Canada Council for the
Arts; the Government of Ontario, through the Ontario Arts Council, Ontario
Creates, and the Ontario Book Publishing Tax Credit. We acknowledge
additional funding provided by the Government of Ontario and the Ontario
Arts Council to address the adverse effects of the novel coronavirus pandemic.

LIBRARY AND ARCHIVES CANADA CATALOGUING IN PUBLICATION

Title: ValHamster / Angela Misri.
Names: Misri, Angela, author.
Identifiers: Canadiana (print) 20210368357 | Canadiana (ebook) 20210368462 |
ISBN 9781770866515 (softcover) | ISBN 9781770866522 (HTML)
Classification: LCC PS8626.I824 V35 2022 | DDC jC813/.6—dc23

United States Library of Congress Control Number: 2021951282

Cover art: Jan Dolby
Interior text design: Tannice Goddard, tannicegdesigns.ca
Manufactured by Friesens in Altona, Manitoba, Canada in February, 2022.

The interior of this book is printed on 100% post-consumer waste recycled paper.
Printed and bound in Canada.

DCB Young Readers
AN IMPRINT OF CORMORANT BOOKS INC.
260 Spadina Avenue, Suite 502, Toronto, ON M5T 2E4
www.dcbyoungreaders.com
www.cormorantbooks.com

In memory of my friend,
Chris Straw.

CHAPTER ONE

I dream of a glorious death.

At least, that's what I've been told heroes should dream of.

I am a warrior, and every day could be my last.

The zombies who rule this world may think they have won the battle, but I have killed more of them than I can count. More than any other mammal here. Certainly more than any hamster before me. And I'm not done yet.

I wish I had a cape.

"Emmy!"

I ignore Diana, the dog with no tail. She's beautiful with her bright orange coat and fox-shaped face, but she's a dog. And dogs can only mean heartbreak.

"Emmy, didn't you hear me calling you?" she asks, bounding up the stairs on her squat legs to where I sit, watching over the battlements of our camp.

"Busy," I say, not even turning to look at her.

"Pickles has called a full meeting," she says, panting slightly at the exertion. See, this is why dogs are trouble. This corgi is so out of shape, she's practically a sausage-shaped zombie snack.

"I'll come," I say, "alone."

I don't have to look at her to know my words hurt. After all, I've lived with dogs since leaving the pet store as a pup two years ago. I know dogs have two moods — crazy happy and wretchedly sad. There is no in between. I stare straight ahead, concentrating on the zombie couple slouching their way through the trees just a few yards away. You could mistake them for a pair of lovebirds the way they move in unison. But as they get closer, you notice the grayness of their skin. The bones that poke through their ragged clothing. And the way they keep chomping at the air as if eating a footlong sandwich.

The humans did something right when they built the fences around this compound. I sit ten feet off the ground, above the zombies, safe from their grasping hands and gnashing teeth. And they are safe from me. For now.

"Oh, okay," Diana says, walking away, taking the stairs one at a time back down. If she had a tail, it would be between her legs. But since she's a former show dog of the corgi breed, her human pet removed her tail when she was just a pup. Supposedly that makes corgis cuter. Humans can be cruel even when they're not undead.

I wait until I can no longer hear her slow, sad movements, counting to seven, and then to seven again. Yes, it's as high as I can count. I start humming my theme music under my breath. A war ballad set to a drumbeat that strikes fear into the hearts of my enemies.

I take the steps down two at a time, because I'm just a hamster and I shouldn't be able to, but I can. I'm flying down them with a speed horses would be jealous of — if horses were smart enough to live through this zombie apocalypse, which, based on my experience, they aren't. I think it has something to do with their eyes being on the sides of their faces rather than facing the front. It's a common issue with prey animals that I do not have because I refuse to be a prey animal. I am a warrior. Lacking a cape.

I tear across the compound and zip up the ramp that leads to The Menagerie, our private enclosure, built by the humans we protect. I do a complete circuit of the roof, sniffing the air and cataloguing the locations of each and every zombie out there. I can't see them all because the sun is going down, but I can hear them, and I can sense them. I glare into the darkness, projecting all my wrath at them as hard as I can. If my eyes were weapons they'd be thunderbolts. Thunderbolts with whirling scimitars.

Once I feel like they've been sufficiently intimidated by my scowls, I skim down through Pal's owl perch to land on the floor of The Menagerie beside Ginger.

"Ack!" the orange cat yelps, nearly jumping out of his white-socked paws. "Where did you come from?"

"Up," I answer nonchalantly, as if I totally didn't mean to scare the fur off him. Warriors don't worry about feelings like surprise or worry. We like to keep everyone on their toes. Speaking of toes, Trip has every toe he owns extended toward the hot stones in the center of our shared space. He just returned from a visit to his gaze of raccoons — two hundred mammals who live about two miles from this location, at a river that features a new beaver dam.

"Icy paws, it's cold out there," the raccoon says by way of explanation, seeing me looking at his toes, "but most of the gaze are out of their hibernation cycle."

I nod, secretly wondering how we will protect two hundred raccoons who live so far outside this compound, but not voicing it. I find that silence usually invites explanation from the more talkative members of this group. I prefer the simmering anger of a long, drawn-out war to the quiet worries of the day. Also, words stress me out. Especially words coming out of my mouth. Words are not action, and without action, emotions seem to bubble to the surface. Better to act than to speak. It's why I speak so little. I'd rather be fighting.

I cast my eyes around to where Hannah, our Abyssinian feline, is hovering at the door that leads from The Menagerie to the human quarters. Her long ears are pointed at the door, waiting for her mate, Pickles, a calico cat with freckles and a terrible name. Pickles is the supposed leader of this group — she brought us all together in the first days of this zombie apocalypse. She was my neighbor, living a few doors down from my pets' home, but I didn't know her until the humans began to turn into zombies. She and Wally were indoor cats, and I was an indoor hamster. Our missions were never meant to cross.

Then Pickles' pet, Connor, didn't come home, and Pickles set out on her quest to find the small human. She left before our block of houses caught fire. Before I was the hamster I am now, back when I had two canine partners named Ralph and Vance. They were Great Danes, dull and slow-witted, but loyal to me and to our human pets. Unlike me, they were outdoor animals, and they went outside every day. They'd return with stories and gossip from our neighborhood, which is how I knew Pickles' and Wally's and Ginger's names. Our pets would take me out of my cage to run around the house with the dogs or to sit in front of the laptop on their laps chewing on celery sticks while we all watched action movies. When those same human pets turned into zombies overnight, the dogs were the ones who destroyed my cage and released me. Ralph threw himself in front of the zombie pets when they lunged for me, and he died protecting me. Vance survived only a few days after that, poisoned by a bite from the zombie who had been our pet. It fell to me to set our house on fire in the hopes that they would make it to ValHamster, the mythic land of warrior souls where we would be reunited someday in all our glory.

I shake my head of those terrible memories, refocusing on Hannah and her vigil.

I admire Pickles and that she was brave enough to leave the safety of her home to find her pet. It's one of the reasons I followed her after the fire, and why I stay here with these mammals. She set out on a noble quest and pursued it regardless of the dangers in front of her, finding Connor and his mother here, at this compound of humans. As a warrior, I was duty bound to help her on her mission to find her pets, but that didn't mean I trusted the humans at this camp any more than I did my own. After all, any human could turn into a zombie at any moment. All it took was a bite.

"Hey, watch it!" exclaims Ginger, batting at the fur around Trip's ankles. Trip yells and falls backwards, using his striped tail to smother the sparks. Ginger shakes his head at his best friend, used to the raccoon's bumbling antics, and Diana sniffs at Trip's ankle. I can't believe this raccoon has lasted as long as he has. I don't think he would have without the support of these cats. Ginger is a short-haired orange tabby who lived in the house next door to mine. He was an outdoor cat, so, unlike Pickles and Wally, I saw him often, prancing through the neighborhood stirring up trouble with his bombastic chatter. He was the one who convinced me of the importance of Pickles' quest and got me to leave the fiery remains of our houses, where I would have been content to be consumed along with Vance and Ralph.

"Thanks, Ginger," Trip says, panting a little at the exertion, staring at his slightly singed fur. Diana, whose canine nose is more sensitive, moves a little further away from the raccoon.

"Are we all here?" Pickles says as she walks into the room with Wally at her side. Wally is followed into The Menagerie by the troop of kittens who train under him, and they scamper about with their characteristic hissing and tumbling sounds. The band of kittens calls themselves the 4077th, and Wally spends far too much energy training them. They are not soldiers. They are just another bunch of mammals we could lose to the zombies.

"Over there, Sergeant Sonar," Wally says, pointing a small black cat at a corner of the room, "and keep the rest of the troop in line or it will be litter duty for a week for all of you."

"Yes, sir," Sonar says, giving a sharp salute and then

leading the rest of the kittens in the direction Wally pointed. Sonar waits until the rest of the kittens are seated before sitting herself, at attention with her ears perked.

"I don't see Pallas," Wally says, coming all the way to the stone pit in the center of the room and sitting down to rub at the bronze star on his collar. The rest of these animals look to Pickles as their leader, but Wally is their strategic brain.

"Present!" Pallas the owl announces, flapping into the room from the window next to his perch. I instinctively get out of the way of my best friend because I know landings are not his forte. He does a slow loop of the stone pit and skims the rough wooden floor before hitting it and rolling into the corner where Pickles and Hannah sleep, disappearing behind the short curtains with a dull bang. This is actually one of his better landings because no one else got hurt.

"I'm fine," he calls, and then trundles out on his two legs. I give him a bit of a dusting off as he walks by me. "Sorry about the mess, Hannah, Pickles."

Hannah flicks her long tail at him in amusement, and they all find spots around the stone pit. I start my usual orbit of the perimeter at a slow jog, keeping an eye on all exits even as my ears are trained on the conversation. I'm not expected to talk if I'm on guard. And I am always on guard. We are, after all, in a camp surrounded by humans, who are surrounded by zombies. Constant vigilance is required.

"Thanks for coming together," Pickles says. "I have camp news I want to share, and I know Trip and Sonar have an update on the tree-to-tree highway out to the dam."

Trip nods, the furry black mask around his eyes crinkling in a way I know means that he's pleased. Sonar is too well trained to move while Wally is watching, but her black whiskers quiver in a way that tells me she has an impressive report to deliver.

"What's the news?" Ginger prompts Pickles.

"A new group of humans will be joining our pets," Pickles answers. "They've been traveling for some time, and they need help."

I slow down behind Pickles to ask, "Trust?"

Pickles nods as I leap over her orange, black, and white tail. "They're being thoroughly checked out, Emmy, by our humans, and Wally's taken a look at them too."

Wally speaks up then. "They're a ragtag bunch with not a lot of organization, but they come bearing lots of human weapons and medicines, which we need. Plus, they had to be tough to make it the distance they did through all that zombie territory. Came all the way across the provincial lines, or so they tell it."

"Any children?" Trip asks.

Pickles and Wally shake their heads. "Sounds like they

lost more than half their group along the way. Only the strongest survived."

One of the 4077th kittens snorts, earning a glare from Sonar. It's a white kitten with a brown stripe between his eyebrows that makes him look like he's always angry. I throw a look at him as well for his disrespect. Meanwhile, Pal wraps his feathered wing around Trip, who looks downcast. It's not that Trip particularly loves baby humans, but some time ago he lost a friend and seems close to tears a lot. A weakness I don't allow in myself. I love no one enough to cry at their loss. You can't. Not in times like these.

"We can't take on any more pets anyway," Ginger says, looking around the group. "We've each got too many assignments as it is."

"They're actually spoken for," Pickles says, exchanging a glance with Wally before seeking out my eyes as I pass behind Trip. "They're traveling with a rabbit and a weasel."

I screech to a halt, my claws digging into Trip's tail.

"Ouch!" he squeals, leaping away from me.

"Weasel?" I spit out, incredulous. Weasels are the sworn enemies of hamsters. Horrid, smelly creatures of deceit and dishonor. Cats have a list of five things they hate the most: rats, water, wet dogs, number four, and cucumbers. Hamsters have one: weasels.

"Uh-oh," murmurs Pal.

"Listen …," Pickles starts to say.

"Weasel," I repeat, walking straight up to the calico cat and glaring up at her.

"Yes, a weasel," she answers, averting her eyes from mine, "but Wally says —"

"Weasels can't be trusted," I say, now directing my ire at the big gray cat.

"I've heard that stereotype before, but have you ever actually met a weasel?" Wally asks, his eyes on the kittens in the corner, trying to maintain order, no doubt, with his disapproving scowl. "I interrogated this one for over an hour, and not only do they seem loyal to their pet humans, but he and the rabbit have skills we could use. They seem to be a package deal."

I cross my arms over my chest, standing on my back paws.

"First of all, the bunny is tough," Wally says. "From her stories, she's killed more zombies than any other mammal I've run into."

If possible, I stiffen even more, and Pal immediately says, "Other than you, Emmy. No one is saying they are better at zombie killing, right, Wally?"

"Of course not," Wally says with a nod that is highly unconvincing and slightly condescending, "and by the Sabre, that weasel can shoot off a smell that would impress a skunk. Could come in handy. Not against the zombies, mind you …"

"That was not a pleasant demonstration by all accounts," Diana says, shaking her head at me.

"There's nothing pleasant about weasels," I mutter under my breath. I've stopped moving long enough to say the important words.

"And he can play dead almost as well as you can, Emmy," Wally points out. "I couldn't even tell if he was breathing, I swear."

He's referring to the time a zombie landed on me and I played dead rather than give the zombie the satisfaction of crushing me. The truth is that I played dead for so long that I thought I might actually *be* dead. It wasn't until these mammals buried me in a grave that I realized playing dead wasn't for me. It made me question the whole concept of a glorious death. Was this death glorious? Had I been heroic enough to reunite with Vance and Ralph in the afterlife? What made a life heroic enough?

"Where are they going to sleep?" asks Ginger, dragging my attention back to the present threat.

Pickles' whiskers quiver before she answers. "We've offered them a spot in The Menagerie, of course."

CHAPTER TWO

I've been betrayed again

I never intended to stay. This compound was a way station on my march against the zombie threat. Somehow, despite all I've endured, I've once again become dependent on other mammals. Obviously, if the powers that be, namely the cats, are letting in random weasels, it's time to get off this hamster wheel and focus on my solo quest of ridding the world of zombies.

Unlike Trip, who wears a fanny pack around his thick waist and has a plastic bag of collected garbage he keeps here in The Menagerie, I have nothing to pack. Warriors travel light. I glance around the room now. Pickles and Hannah are in their corner; Ginger, Wally, Sonar, and the kittens of the 4077th are snuggled around the stone pit. Pal and Trip are out on their nightly foraging run, as nocturnal animals are apt to do in the twilight hours. Pal tried to talk me into coming with them, no doubt to try to soften the blow of the cats inviting a weasel into our midst, but I declined. He's a smart friend. He understood I needed time to myself to mull everything over. I'm hoping he comes to the same conclusion as me about the weasel and leaves this place. I will find him out in the wilderness. We will fight the zombies side by side until the end.

The dog. Where is the dog?

I dash up to Pal's perch and out onto the roof to peer down into the compound.

Human guards walk the fence line on their raised platforms, and the bonfire they maintain in the east end of the enclosed camp provides a feeble light. If I had a cape it would be billowing in the wind that gusts around me.

I squint into the darkness, annoyed that I can't see Diana, and equally annoyed that I care. I wonder if she's out on patrol with the humans. Sometimes, she or Ginger goes out with the guards, walking the circuit around the compound. I have never volunteered for that duty because the humans walk far too slowly. I work alone. They must understand my preference because I have never been asked.

"Whatever," I say through my teeth, turning to the tree closest to The Menagerie. Trip is the architect in charge of the tree-to-tree highway leading from The Menagerie in this compound all the way to the river, where the beaver dam and the gaze of raccoons are located. I understand the concept, of course — it's a safe way to travel back and forth above the heads of the zombies — but to me, it's just another point of failure. Another way for mammals around me to be lost to the zombie threat.

"Not my problem anymore," I grunt, refusing to risk that loss again, and I zip up the ramp that leads into the tree. It creaks under my paws, and I have a second to wonder how it carries Trip's additional weight if it can't even handle mine.

"Where are you going?"

I whip around, teeth bared, ready to do battle.

Diana stands on the lower end of the ramp, looking up at me at the top.

I slowly retract my claws from the wood I've dug into. "Out."

"Out where?" she presses, coming up the ramp a little. So that was why it was creaking behind me: her added weight.

Heroes don't lie, and I want to cut this short, so I say, "Out. Forever."

"You're leaving?" she asks, her voice high and surprised. "Is this about the weasel?"

I hate that my actions are this well known, and that it is this animal, a dog, who knows too much. Aren't cats the ones who are supposed to be curious?

"You weren't even going to say goodbye?"

I shake my head. It's not like the cats checked with me

before inviting in a known enemy. Or like my supposed best friend, the owl, stopped them. Again, the dog seems to anticipate my answers.

"You haven't even met them, Emmy," she says. "Don't you think you should talk to them yourself before you write them off and abandon your family?"

"Family?" I spit out. How few words do I need to make my point without revealing my hurt? "Weasels not family."

"Not them," she says, stepping even closer so that she's only about a hamster-length from me. "Us. We're your family. And you're leaving us behind."

I grit my teeth against the vision of two Great Danes that rises in my mind. "Emmy has no family."

"Fine," Diana answers, anger displacing the surprise in her voice, her ears actually flattening a little on her fox-shaped head, "but don't say you don't care what happens to us, because you have rescued more animals than I can count. Me included."

I won't deny that. Warriors rescue helpless animals. It's part of our reason for being. But these animals aren't helpless. They're just gullible, to take in weasels. And if they're choosing a weasel over me then it's just a matter of time before I lose one of them to his vile machinations. I'm not sticking around for a betrayal like that. It's my pets turning into zombies all over again.

"Shouldn't you at least make sure they're not dangerous before you leave?" she suggests, sliding backwards down the ramp. She can't actually turn around on the ramp: it's too narrow, and she's too wide. "I think you owe us that."

I open my mouth to deny owing her anything at all, but the way she's looking at me with the wind rippling her fur reminds me too much of Vance. I owe my life to two dogs, and it's a debt I can never repay. And a pain I will never subject myself to again. But I'm not one to shirk my responsibilities.

Instead of answering her question, I prefer to act. I run right under her, brushing her belly with my ears and bouncing off the ramp behind her. I can take care of this before I go.

"Hey!" she calls, but I'm already scampering down from the roof, down to the fence line to run along the wooden perimeter.

New animals and humans are quarantined outside the border fence of the camp. That's the protocol instituted by Wally and his pet, and one I highly approve of. That means these new humans will have set up their tents on the east wall of our compound, directly below the guard tower, so we can keep an eye on them while they go through the entry process. I run along the battlements, around barrels and rope and uncut logs. Two of our humans, Ginger's pets I think, stand on guard above the tents, and I sneak between their legs to look out over the fence.

A small fire is burning between the tents, and three humans I don't know or trust sit around it. They've put up a rudimentary fence around their tents, a bunch of sharpened logs pointing outwards like teeth stuck into the ground. The humans have discovered that the average zombie is too stupid to dodge the sharp ends and will invariably impale itself on the logs, stopping the zombie in its tracks.

I eye the distance from our ten-foot-high fence to the roof of the first tent and decide to risk it. I hurl myself over the fence edge, imagining a red cape fluttering majestically behind me, and land with a bounce on the tent. I flatten immediately lest I be seen, but neither the humans around the fire nor the ones back on the fence have noticed. These tents are ragged, with silvery duct tape pressed along the seams and patching several rips. It's about half original tent material and half tape. I slide my body to the edge of the tarp, avoiding sticky tape, and ride a cord down to the ground, landing soundlessly beside the tent.

"Stop right there," says a voice behind me.

Instead of obeying the command, I roll to the side and come up, teeth and claws bared, to see a rabbit about twice my size pointing a sharpened stick at me. I hiss at her, and her almond-shaped eyes narrow.

"You're about two seconds from being skewered, rodent," she hisses at me.

I grab the sharp end of the stick, and we wrestle for it, hissing and growling at each other. I won't let go: I've got my front paws and my jaw locked on it, and the rabbit can't shake me loose.

"Diana, what are you doing here?" I hear a human voice say somewhere behind us, but I ignore it. I will not surrender. I'd die first.

A skinny weasel slithers out from under the tent, and his eyes go wide when he sees us. "Spike? Holy whiskers, Spike, stop!"

The rabbit growls in response, "Back off, Wheels, I've got this. I told you I'd find us a home."

"Both of you, stop!" barks Diana from the fence above us.

The weasel steps close enough for me to see that he's shaking with fear.

"Please, Spike, stop," he begs the rabbit, scratching at his nose. "We'll get thrown out of the camp, and I've done the calculations — we won't survive another week out there with the zombies. Please!"

The weasel's pathetic sniveling is the perfect distraction for the rabbit. With a grunt, I yank the stick free and flip it around in my paws so that I'm pointing the sharp end at the rabbit and the weasel. She hisses, looking around for another weapon, but the weasel surprises both of us by stepping in front of her, his front paws raised. He's tall when he stands on his hind paws like this.

"We're not here to hurt you," he says to me slowly, as if I'm a dull-witted pigeon. His voice is quaking as much as his scrawny body. "We talked to a cat named Wally this afternoon. Ask him. Ask your cats."

"Do I look like a cat, weasel?" I hiss at him, pressing the pointy end of the stick into his concave chest.

He winces but holds his ground, and my estimation of this weasel goes up a notch. That said, it was pretty low to begin with. Like, underside of the litter paper low.

"Don't, Emmy, please," Diana says from behind me, her concerned voice grating on my nerves. The heat of battle is fading, but I still want to run this weasel through. I should. Just on principle.

The rabbit finds a rock and grips it in her paw, panting heavily.

That's when a zombie rips his way out of the tent right next to us.

Just in case you're wondering how I know it's a zombie and not a regular live human, he's chomping on his own arm like it's a turkey drumstick. He's also covered in strips of duct tape, with shreds of the tent trailing after him, which is slowing him down. But not enough.

The fog of war falls over my eyes, and I can barely hear the screams of the humans or Diana's yelps from above us on the fence.

"Good hunting!" I yell and launch myself at the zombie, thrusting the pointy stick through his bare foot as hard as I can, staking him to the soft forest floor. He stops, pulling at his foot, so I duck into his pant leg, climbing up his hairy leg as quickly as I can. A zombie's head is its only vulnerable spot, other than burning them in one of my bonfires, so I know I have to somehow detach this undead human's head from his body. I pull myself out of the pants and head up the torso, passing the bite that must have turned this human from alive to undead. I smell something terrible and realize the weasel has entered the battle, and he is doing more damage to those of us who have working noses than to this zombie. Zombies don't smell. They just eat. I wish this zombie would eat the weasel and solve my problems.

I yank myself out of the zombie's shirt and bound onto his shoulder as he stumbles around, pulling his staked foot free and lurching toward a female human cowering in front of him, duct tape waving off his arms like ribbons.

"Haaaaa!" yells the rabbit, leaping impossibly high and landing on the shoulder opposite me.

The zombie starts slapping at the rabbit, but she

dodges his clumsy hand and throws me one end of a long piece of barbed wire. "Go!" she yells.

I immediately grasp her plan. I loop myself around the zombie's neck, and the rabbit goes the opposite way so that we're both running around and around the zombie's head, wrapping barbed wire around his neck. Now we're on opposite shoulders again, and without needing to be asked, I pull tight on my end of the barbed wire.

The rabbit does the same, leaning back so far off the zombie's shoulder that she falls out of sight, her end of the wire taut with her body weight.

The zombie lurches as humans fire their guns at it from the compound fence above us. My ears ring with the deafening sounds, but the zombie swings toward the weasel, who is frozen in place on the ground in front of us. His strategy reminds me of Trip's technique when dealing with zombies — equally useless. He starts leaning to the side, signaling he's going to try the playing-dead thing again. Only this time he might end up the real kind of dead rather than the fake kind.

"No, Wheels! Run!" Spike yells at the weasel as she swings like a pendulum from the end of the barbed wire. She's getting wound up in the duct tape hanging off the zombie's back.

Her words change his strategy, and he takes off into the forest at top speed, our zombie lumbering after him.

I leap off the shoulder as well, gripping the barbed

wire, but even our combined weights hanging off each side of this zombie aren't enough to remove the zombie's head from his neck. We're flailing around on the ends of our wire, bouncing along as he bashes his way through the rudimentary fence.

"Not working," I yell at the rabbit. "Let go!"

A muffled "Mmmph!" is all I hear in response.

Still holding on to my end of the barbed wire, I let out a battle trill and scamper along the zombie's torso like a mountain climber scaling the side of the rock face. I come around the zombie's side as he barrels into a tree, and I get a smack to the side of the head. Now I'm seeing stars. I shake my head and finally get a glimpse of the rabbit. She's wrapped up like a mummy in duct tape. She's not even holding on to the barbed wire anymore; instead, she's using all four paws and her teeth to try to get free of the sticky tape.

The weasel darts left, so our zombie-ride does the same, and I feel the sting of a branch in my side. I ignore it, using the momentum to hurl myself onto the shoulder above the rabbit. She's got one paw free, so I reach down and grab it.

I pull as hard as I can and manage to pull her head free. Her eyes are as huge and round as shields, but she's not scared, just determined.

"Pull!" I growl down at her, but she's shaking her head, trying to pull her paw free of mine.

"What are you doing?!" I yell, but she yanks her paw out of mine and pushes down the tape around her mouth.

"Look out!" she yells, pointing with her one free paw.

I lean out and see what she's freaking out about. The zombie is barreling toward the edge of a cliff.

"Jump!" she yells up at me.

The zombie stoops as he runs and grabs the weasel, who shrieks piteously and goes limp in response, and I realize this could be the end. Two warriors vanquishing a zombie and a cowardly weasel. But who will fight tomorrow? Who will protect my friends back at the camp when we are gone? Oddly, I don't hear the screams as we run out of cliff and start to fall. I hear dogs barking. I imagine that a long red cape is billowing out behind me, following my ascent to ValHamster and to the two Great Danes who loved me.

CHAPTER THREE

Water is lapping at my face.

Wait, water doesn't smell like bacon treats.

My eyes snap open to see Diana's face above me, her tongue hanging out.

"You're alive," she breathes, backing up a bit. She's ankle deep in water. "He's dead," she says, pointing with her nose at the zombie body I'm still lying on. His head is noticeably missing, and as I scan back up the cliffside I see why. It's hanging by barbed wire from a branch sticking out halfway down the cliff.

With an effort I'm determined not to show, I pull myself off the still torso of my fallen enemy, feeling every bump and bruise. A long scratch runs the length of my body and throbs faintly.

"Careful, Emmy," Diana says. "You fell a long way."

I grunt in response and then ask, "How did you get here?"

She shrugs and says, "I was following you, out of the camp and through the woods. I was barking, trying to show our humans which way the zombie was going, but they didn't follow. I think there were more zombies back at the camp."

I nod, noticing for the first time that the rabbit is lying on her back in the shallows of the river, still wrapped in duct tape. The weasel is soaking wet, working feverishly to revive her, raising her paws above her head and pressing on her chest rhythmically. I instinctively look to the skies, sure I will see Pal searching for us on wobbly wings, but the sky is empty of low-flying birds.

"Zombie grabbed you too?" I ask Diana as I stumble over to crouch at the rabbit's side.

"No. I saw you go over the cliff, and I jumped," Diana says, following me. "It's not that high, but I aimed for the deeper water. I think you and that zombie hit every rock on the way down."

I'm surprised that she leapt after us, but remembering Vance and Ralph and their extreme loyalty, I shouldn't be. I guess I'm startled that Diana feels that kind of loyalty to me. It worries me. I don't like being responsible for that kind of devotion. It will lead to pain. It always does.

"Come on, Spike," the weasel is saying over and over. Tears are falling from his eyes, and I'm shocked to feel an emotional response bubbling up as well. This is very bad. I don't even know half these mammals. It brings back memories of losing Vance and Ralph and the pain of standing over them while monsters hammered at the door. Shake it off, Emmy! You're a warrior. Think of battle. Think of this victory!

Diana licks at the rabbit's paws, trying to do her part, and I just stand there staring, lost in memories. I'm a fighter, not a healer. I feel anger rise up inside me. It's not appropriate, I know that. But it's what I'm feeling, and I prefer it to the sadness. Spike fought well. She should be allowed to die well. Anyway, this is all the weasel's fault for running pell-mell through the forest and leading us off a cliff. I've actually opened my mouth to bark that at the weasel when Spike sputters, coughing out river water.

"Oh, thank the Wolverine," the weasel says, bursting into tears. Diana grins and wraps a paw around him, looking at me in triumph. I back away from the scene, scanning the trees for possible threats. I don't want to feel this unity. I don't want to feel like a family. I don't want to feel anything but the fire and fury that carried me out of the camp.

Spike struggles to sit up, but the tape is still holding her tight.

"Here, take this end," Diana says, pulling one end of the duct tape with her teeth and dipping it in the water, getting it wet so that it releases from the rabbit's coat.

Spike winces as Wheels pulls the other end of the tape, her fur stuck to it.

"Sorry, sorry, sorry," I hear Wheels say as he and Diana pull on the tape.

I do a complete circuit of the beach while they unwind the rabbit from the duct tape. It's a human-built park, peppered with wooden benches and metal garbage cans. We've come across them before in our travels. I discover that except for a family of ravens, we are alone. Good. But where is Pal? Surely he knows we're missing? We can't have been that hard to track from the camp to this cliff. My body feels like we hit every rock and cracked every branch on the way down.

I slow to a walk beside the zombie body, glaring at it, projecting curse words through my eyeballs. This zombie was one of the newcomers at our camp, proving once again that all humans are a zombie risk. Better to avoid them all — alive or undead.

I stop next to where the rabbit, the weasel, and the dog now sit, on the beach, out of the water. The rabbit is shaking like a leaf, whether from shock or cold, I can't tell.

"We need a fire," Diana says, looking at me. She knows how much I like fire. It's a powerful weapon in my arsenal.

I dash into the forest, scooping up little bits of moss and dry twigs. I slow to a stop near a bench with a small bronze plaque that reads, "'Being deeply loved by someone gives you strength, while loving someone deeply gives you courage.' — Lao Tzu."

I snort. Sounds like something Pickles would quote at me out of one of her books. That's the opposite of a warrior's creed. Love makes you weak. I hate feeling weak. I snort again, carrying the moss and twigs back to the beach. I stack everything up and sit back. I still need something to light the fire. I wish Trip were here. He always carries a few matches in the bottom of his bottomless fanny pack. And if he doesn't have the matches himself, he usually negotiates something from the wildlife around him.

"Weasel," I snap, the name tasting like ash in my mouth. "Ravens."

"Huh?" Wheels answers, ambling over to stand beside me, dripping on my perfect pile of kindling. I shove him back so the river water isn't a threat to my wood and say, "Ravens. Ask for matches."

He looks up at the trees of the forest confusedly. I'm losing my patience with this stupid weasel. All these words are stressing me out. I'm not a negotiator. And his main skill is deception, so he should get along well with ravens.

Diana calls out, "Ask the ravens if they will trade for matches, Wheels, so we can start a fire and warm Spike up."

"Don't need it," Spike chatters through her teeth, exactly how a warrior should.

"Oh, sure," the weasel says, still not moving in the direction of the trees.

"Here, I'll come with you," Diana offers, nudging the weasel into the forest with her long nose. "Where are the ravens, Emmy?"

I point silently at the nest I passed earlier and watch Diana escort Wheels. I wonder if I should follow in case the weasel turns on her. It's in his nature, after all.

"Hey, is that dog safe?" Spike asks me.

I look back at the rabbit, who is still shivering but has moved to sit beside the twigs in anticipation of a fire.

"The weasel," I correct automatically.

"No, the dog," she answers, giving me a weird look. "I've been with Wheels for months. I don't know that dog from a hole in the ground. And I'm a rabbit. I know holes in the ground."

"Trust dogs over weasels," I reply, feeling like I'm educating a newborn pup.

Spike squints at the trees, trying to catch sight of them. "I've never spoken to a dog before, and they usually chase mammals like us."

Okay, this requires actual important words, maybe even a full conversation. "Diana jumped off a cliff. For us."

"For you, I'm sure," Spike corrects me. "But if you will vouch for this dog, I trust you."

She shivers and scratches at the patch of missing fur on her arm, and notices me noticing. "Doesn't hurt."

I grunt my approval, because that is what a warrior should say. She may not know that weasels are not to be trusted, but Spike has qualities I admire. Like courage and loyalty. Maybe I don't need to strike out on my own after all. Once Pal shows up, this could be a trio I could trust.

"You fought well," I say.

"I did, but you fought better," she replies, her eyes returning to meet mine, proud and bright. "Next time, I will not be trapped by tape that way."

I wave that away. The tools of warfare can't be predicted. It's your response to them that shows your honor. And her response was to fight to the death.

"You didn't jump free when you had the chance," she points out.

"ValHamster doesn't welcome cowards," I reply, watching the weasel and the dog return and scanning the area behind them suspiciously.

"ValHamster?"

"The land of dead warriors," I reply immediately, "where the brave live forever on sunny battlefields filled with …"

"Filled with?" she asks when I stop short.

What is the battlefield filled with? Enemies? Heroes? Pillows? I don't know that I've ever thought all the way through the mythical promise of ValHamster. I am saved from answering a question I have never really thought about by the weasel's announcement.

"We got them," the weasel declares, waving two matches in the air triumphantly.

Diana is all smiles beside him, her tongue hanging out of her mouth. "Wheels is almost as good at trading as Trip is. We got these for a steal. All they wanted was to know where we were camped."

"Uh-oh," says Spike, her shivers stopping as she scans the sky.

I leap forward to cut the distance between me and the weasel in half.

I hear Spike's warning as I dive the rest of the distance and land on the weasel, his eyes as round as shields. I knock the air out of the skinny mammal just as a feathered black blur skims over us. The weasel is squirming underneath me, but I grab the matches and hold them between our bodies.

"Bah! Begone, fowl creature!" yells Spike, leaping high and smacking at the air.

I feel Diana place herself over us, shielding us both with her sausage-shaped body. She barks up at the ravens threateningly, and they disperse, cursing us.

"They're leaving," she says from above us.

"Watch them," I growl, wresting the matches from the weasel and rolling out from under the dog. I have the fire lit before the ravens have a chance to make another attack. Spike pulls a slim stick out, brandishing the fiery end at the sky.

"But ... we traded ..." Wheels sputters to Diana as he too crawls out from under her. I want to snap at him, but Spike beats me to it.

"You can't trust ravens, Wheels," she says, her eyes on the skies. They're so angry and blue that they're practically spitting javelins.

"Then why'd you send me out to trade with them?" Wheels asks me.

I stoke the fire a little before answering, the sound of crackling and the smell of burning calming me, as it always does. "Ravens like things. They keep the things."

Betrayal runs deep in those birds. And I probably hate betrayal more than anything. More than zombies, even. Maybe I do have a list of things I hate the most: weasels, betrayal, zombies.

Spike nods, wringing out her long ears sensibly away from the fire, the stick at her feet and within quick reach. She's starting to dry out nicely, her cotton tail puffing back up to its normal roundish shape.

"You can trade with them, but you have to be prepared for them to snatch things back?" asks Wheels, scratching at his nose furiously. "How is that a fair trade?"

"To a raven, taking it back is the second half of the trade deal," Spike says. "Anything they can grab back is fair trade."

"And you knew that?" Diana asks me, sitting too close for comfort.

"A steal is never a good deal," I mumble, edging closer to the rabbit.

CHAPTER FOUR

Spike and I take shifts watching over the other two animals. The truth is, I don't trust her weasel, and she doesn't trust my dog. But fighting side by side in battle the way we did means we trust each other. I'm looking to the sky more than I would like to admit. Pal should have found us by now. I push down my worry that the camp has been overrun by zombies with an almost physical effort. I can't believe I've gotten this attached to anyone again, but Pal should be here. It doesn't make sense. I gather firewood and keep the fire going all night, its meager light casting my shadow large against the trees. I imagine that I look terrifying to the neighborhood squirrels and chipmunks. I like it. Maybe I don't need that cape.

I wake to the sound of whittling. I blink the sleep from my eyes to see Spike creating a new sharpened stick from the one she planted beside the fire. She's using her powerful front teeth like a wood chipper. Obviously, she got her name from her preferred weapon. I respect that.

"Sun's coming up," she says, pointing an ear to the east, "and you grind your teeth when you sleep."

I nod, my stomach growling.

"I got some mushrooms for us," she says, pushing forward a leaf full of vegetables. Normally I would turn my nose up at mushrooms, but warriors, like a good fire, need fuel. I force myself to swallow two of the mushrooms, hating every slimy piece, if only to gather the energy to find tastier food. Pal and Trip are the best at spying out good food — an anthill filled with six-legged queen-worshipping drones or a poorly defended honeycomb. Foraging is not generally the work of warriors ... unless it's dangerous. But I suppose if I am striking out on my own, I'd better improve this skill.

I stretch and then bolt for the forest behind us.

I never walk when I can run.

I run in a semicircle around our position on the beach, cataloguing animals, potential food, and probable enemies. I pass the rabbit, who is now jabbing the pointy stick at the air in a practiced kata that involves flipping in the air sideways. On my second orbit, I slow down to glare at the ravens' nest before scampering halfway up the tree and out on a branch. I scan for zombies. Nothing. Pal still hasn't passed by in the sky. I don't like that. I also don't like that I don't like that.

I zoom back down the tree, grabbing a few bugs along the way and popping them in my mouth like candy.

I hit the ground at a run, scaring a couple of chipmunks, and I head straight for a crab apple tree I spied on my first pass. I have to walk back to our base camp dragging a large leaf stacked with crab apples, but the way Spike grins at me makes the slower pace worthwhile.

"Perfect," she says, thrusting her stick into an apple and holding it over the fire. "It sweetens the crab out of the apple," she explains.

I arrange the rest of the apples around the fire. Then I step back and mimic her kata, kicking the air with a force that should impress. It's all about follow-through. You have to mean to kick what you kick.

"Karate?" I ask curiously. I watched a lot of fight movies beside my pet, on his laptop. My favorite were the Thor movies, obviously. But I take the best fighting elements from each as part of my warrior development.

She shakes her head. "My pet was an Amazon."

I've heard of the Amazons, of course, but thought they were fiction, or at least extinct. Like the Vikings of old. My heroes.

"Not a real Amazon, of course," Spike continues, now placing a mushroom on the end of her stick and roasting it over the fire, "but she had every book on the

Amazons, and she practiced their culture like a religion. She developed this kata out of her readings, and I learned from my cage."

She replaces the cooked mushroom on the leaf and moves on to the next fungus.

"Amazon survived?" I ask.

Spike rotates the mushroom a few times over the flames before answering. "Lost her in the first few days after the zombies appeared."

I suspected as much. "Fighting?"

"To the end," Spike answers, pride resonating in the straightness of her whiskers. "A warrior's death."

The weasel rolls over in his sleep, no doubt smelling a convenient meal beside a fire some other mammal built and protected all night. Typical of the species to be so selfish.

"Weasel?" I ask, trying not to spit out the question. Out of respect for the rabbit, of course.

Spike glances over to where Wheels is sleeping fitfully. "My pet saved his from a whole herd of zombies. I took on her responsibilities after she was gone."

I shake my head at the sleeping animal. Of course, the pet of a weasel would be as useless as the weasel itself.

"How about you?" Spike asks.

"Betrayed," I reply. That word best covers how I find myself here. First betrayed by our pets in the house I burned down. Then betrayed by the cats who gave away my home to this weasel.

"By …?"

I watch Diana slowly blink her eyes open before I answer. "Humans. The pets. They became zombies."

Spike nods as if this is a story she has heard before. "Your pets turned on you. I'm so sorry."

I shrug to prove I'm over it, passing on what I have learned. "Don't get attached. Don't get betrayed."

Diana stretches languidly, shaking off sand, and turns to look at us, prompting me to underline my plans with more words than I usually would. "I travel now. Travel far. Away from … attachments. Fight. Win. Fight more."

"For honor and glory?" Spike asks with a grin.

"For honor and glory," I agree, happy she at least understands.

"How do we get back?" Diana asks, her snout tilted up, looking at the top edge of the cliff we leapt from. The sun is fully up, and we are better able to see our situation.

Diana takes a few tentative steps up the cliff, trying to maintain her balance, but slides back down with a yelp. Spike bounces up the cliffside a bit, but at an angle, trying to find a less vertical way to climb up. She makes it up almost halfway before she loses a foothold and tumbles back down.

"Ouch," she says, wincing.

"Be careful, Spike," Diana says, helping her up.

I think I could burrow up if I had to, but it would take some time, and it would need to be a very wide tunnel to fit Diana. Spike stretches and then leaps up the nearest tree. If Trip were here, he would throw us down a rope and we could use that to climb up. Or we could grasp the rope in our teeth and be pulled up by Trip and his raccoon friends.

The weasel is awake now too and scratching in the sand next to him with a twig. The sound is starting to seriously annoy me.

"The cliff extends as far as I can see in both directions," Spike yells from a branch about thirteen feet above the ground. The way she hopped up the tree from branch to branch would have made a monkey proud.

I don't need to return to the camp. I was on my way out anyway. But there is no way I'm starting this new expedition with Diana. No dogs. Not for me. Never again. And that means the corgi at least will have to be returned to the humans. The weasel too, if that means he is out of my life. And maybe I need to make sure The Menagerie is still standing. If I am going anyway. I say none of this aloud, of course. I'm watching the trees for movement because no one else is. An owl swoops by, and my heart leaps, thinking it might be Pallas. No. This owl is huge. Three times as big as our owl. The owl, I mean. He's not mine. Best friends don't let weasels move in, and warriors don't need friends. We have allies and we have enemies.

"Upstream or downstream, Wheels?" Spike calls down from her tree.

The weasel either doesn't hear (I've heard that they're notoriously deaf) or is too lazy to answer. I believe the first because all that scratching in the sand would drive a mammal with normal hearing crazy.

Diana pads over to sit beside me. I wish she wouldn't — it reminds me of when Ralph would snuggle up next to me after a big meal, all warm and content. "What do you think, Emmy?"

I shrug because I don't really have a directional opinion, but I say, "Wait here for Pal to find us. Might work. Defend this position." If Pal shows up, he can join me or he and Diana can escort these random mammals back without me.

"The low ground?" she asks. "Aren't you always telling us to get to higher ground?"

I'm actually surprised enough to make eye contact with the dog. She was listening? She remembered that? Vance and Ralph were loyal to a fault, to their very last moments, but I don't think they ever listened to a word I said to them. It's why my language skills are so sparse. They taught me that actions were more important than words. I didn't really speak until after I met Pickles and her band of chatty cats. And then, I didn't want to speak because words were so heavy with meaning. Every word felt heavy. And sad. Even now, it's not like anyone listens to me. But this dog does.

"Yes," I reply, because strategically Diana's right, "but Pal sees us on beach. Not in trees."

Diana starts scanning the skies hopefully, sniffing at the air as I regard her graceful profile.

"I don't smell any of our friends," she says finally, looking downcast.

"Not even Pal?"

"No," she says. "I know Pal's scent very well. He's not here."

I trust a dog's sense of smell. "Zombies?" I ask.

She sniffs again. "Upstream, I think."

I bare my teeth in that direction. I'll need a bigger fire. And maybe some rope.

Spike, meanwhile, is hopping lithely down the tree a branch at a time, landing with an impressive thud in the sand right between Diana and me.

"Zombies?" she asks, picking up her pointy stick.

"Upstream," I reply with a grin.

"We need to head downstream," announces Wheels. What?

Diana asks before I can, "Why, Wheels?"

"According to what I can remember of my pet's map," Wheels says, glancing at the dead zombie and then away with a shudder, "there's a human tunnel that cuts through this cliffside that should lead us back to your camp."

Now we're supposed to trust a zombie's map and the word of a weasel. I don't think so.

"We go upstream," I announce, "kill zombies, find higher ground, stay visible to Pal."

"You want to go *toward* the zombies?" Wheels squeaks, finally stepping away from his scratching in the sand.

"Kill them first," I answer, looking to Spike for support.

"Spike, you can't agree with this ... hamster ... we have to get back to the camp," Wheels sputters. "Diana, please?"

Diana walks around the map in the sand, being careful not to disturb it with her paw prints. "Are you sure about this tunnel, Wheels?"

"I'm sure that's where it was on the map," he answers, scratching at his nose. "I've never actually seen it."

"If we go upstream, will we find the camp?" Diana presses, her eyes on the map. "This looks like a shorter route back, up here, across a bridge."

"That bridge is made of rope, strung between cliffs," Wheels says. "The tunnel is made of concrete and on the ground."

"Faster and kill zombies," I say, tamping out the fire with sand.

"Sounds like a plan," Diana says, nodding at me. I pick up the second match we almost lost to the ravens

and slip it carefully into Diana's collar. She holds still for
me to secure it. We start to walk away, me in front, circling
Diana as she sniffs the air. Spike seems to be thinking,
tapping the ground with one paw, and Wheels is basically sputtering and pointing at his map. It would be a
shame to leave such a resourceful Amazonian warrior
behind. But I don't like to change my mind once I've
declared my intentions. Wordy negotiations are for cats
and humans. Warriors don't waver. We act.

We're about six feet away when I hear Spike and
Wheels break into a heated argument where we left them.
Wheels is gesticulating wildly, and Spike is shaking her
head so hard her ears are flapping against her face.

"They'll follow," Diana says as I pass her in my orbit.
"It's their only choice."

"Why?" I ask.

"Because you're their best chance of making it back
to camp," she answers. "I know that. Spike knows that.
Wheels needs a minute to understand that."

"Don't want to help a weasel," I say.

"But you will," she answers, smiling at me, "because
warriors save the helpless. Even if they don't like them."

I sigh, because she's not wrong.

"Emmy, have you thought any more about —"

"Still leaving."

"But, you've talked to Wheels now," she says. "He's
harmless. He's not the best zombie fighter …"

I snort at her understatement.

"But he's not the monster you thought he was," she continues, her tone adamant. "You have to admit that."

I force my eyes from the sky. I'm not admitting anything. And I'm so not looking for Pal. I push all of it away. I wish I could push these animals away as easily as my feelings.

"But what's the plan then? Abandon us?"

Spike hops to catch up with us. "I'll take the rear," she announces.

I nod, showing my respect for her skills by stopping my usual orbit and just leading the expedition from the front of the company, something I've never done with the cats. I don't look, but I assume the weasel is along for the ride. At least there will be no guilt or pain when the weasel gets eaten by a zombie. I won't let him cause the death of Spike or Diana. Maybe that is my mission. Kill zombies. Return mammals. Lose weasels.

Forget the cape, I deserve a halo.

CHAPTER FIVE

"Stop," Diana says, her nose high in the air.

I immediately do as she says and cast my eyes over the forest beside us, looking for what she can already smell.

"Zombies?" the weasel whispers in a shaking voice from behind Diana.

Diana sniffs again, a frown on her face. "No, something alive. I don't recognize it."

"Where?" Spike asks, her sharpened stick in her paws and pointed at the forest.

"There," I say, pointing at a huge animal casually walking into the river ahead of us.

"What …," Wheels sputters, "… what is that?"

"Bear," I reply, squinting at the animal.

"A bear," Diana repeats, wonder in her voice. "I've never seen one."

I've never seen one in real life either, but my pet's

sister had many stuffed versions of this creature on her pink bed. This one is less cute.

I'M ASSESSING THE SITUATION. I don't have time for wonder. The bear is nonchalantly batting fish out of the water with practiced skill. He's a physical threat to be sure, but he seems happy with fish as a meal. We should go around him.

"Do you think we could trade for some fish?" Diana asks, licking her lips.

"Are you looking at the same monster I am?" Wheels demands. "The one with claws the size of your hamster?"

We are all looking at it now, so we have a clear view of the putrefied zombie who sits up in the middle of the river-bed next to the bear's fishing ground.

I'm running before Diana can yell for me to stop, my brain already ticking through the ways I can win this fight. Obviously, this zombie is too wet to burn in a fire. But those rocks the bear is standing on look uneven enough to bash a zombie head. As long as you take out the head, the zombie is done for.

"Run!" Diana yells, catching up to me, the rabbit hopping at her side. "You! Bear! Run!"

Even from the shore, I can see the bear looking at the zombie stupidly, his eyes half open, his mouth still chewing on his fishy meal.

"Huh?" the bear says, his gaze swinging slowly to us, a

band of crazed mammals running toward him.

"Stupid bear," Spike and I say at the same time, not slowing down.

"Hibernation," Diana barks. "You've been hibernating."

"Get lost!" the bear says to the zombie (and maybe by extension to us); the zombie is now groaning his way out of the deeper part of the river, his arms reaching for the bear.

"He doesn't know about zombies," Diana says to me, her eyes wide. "Emmy, he's been hibernating!"

The fact that the bear is grossly unaware of his imminent death is just another problem we can't solve. Being unprepared for the coming war is his fault, not my problem. I had to learn fast. We all did. If life were fair, Vance and Ralph would still be alive. If life were fair, I wouldn't have had to leave The Menagerie because of overly trusting do-gooder felines.

But this zombie will be my revenge. All zombies are my revenge. The only question is if it will happen before or after the bear becomes a meal for the undead.

The bear smacks at the zombie's outstretched arm, and the arm flies off and into the river. The zombie doesn't care, he keeps walking forward. The bear's eyes widen. Maybe he's starting to figure out this might not be a problem he can solve with pure brawn. I screech to a stop on the beach a couple yards behind the zombie.

"What's wrong with it?" the bear demands, dodging the zombie and smacking it in the leg. The zombie's leg is now bent at a weird angle, but he's determined to taste bear. He drags himself though the water with one arm and one working leg.

"It's dead," Diana says, walking into the water up to her ankles, "but if it bites you, you will die."

"What?" the bear says, backing up out of the water. "What are you talking about? It's dead, but it'll bite me?"

"Can we talk about this later?" Diana barks loudly, frustration clear in her voice. "Just run!"

The bear hesitates. I don't think he's ever run from another mammal in his life. Not with that girth. He reminds me of Trip. But bigger and slower. I get ready to let out a loud battle trill when Spike whistles sharply through her long front teeth.

The zombie twists to see us, and I grin savagely. Perfect.

"Good hunting!" I hiss at the world.

Diana runs around behind us, and the zombie slouches his way to our side of the beach.

"Rocks, Spike," I say, not taking my eyes off the human monster for a minute.

Spike nods and says, "Bear, we'll need your weight when we get him down."

"My what?" he demands, sounding offended.

"Crush him. Don't bite," I hiss through my teeth.

There's no chance for more conversation as the zombie struggles upright on his one working leg, and the battle is on.

Spike leaps into the air, her sharpened stick poised, and slams the weapon into the zombie's face. He swats at her as she jumps onto his head, kicking at his skull with her powerful hind legs. I run up the zombie's leg, heading for the belt. I grab one end of the worn leather and leap back off the dead human, pulling the belt as I go. The zombie loses his balance and comes crashing down behind me, his head smacking into the rocks, just as I planned. The bear gives a massive bellow and throws himself onto the zombie. We jump free just in time.

"Don't bite it!" Diana yells, but she's too late: the bear is overtaken with battle furor now.

Spike lands beside me with an astonished look on her face. I'd like to say I was surprised, but those bears on that pink bedspread in my old house weren't just cuter. They were also way smarter than this one.

CHAPTER SIX

"I should have explained it," Diana says again.

She's inconsolable. The bear is over it. He's back in the river, smacking fish out of the water and onto the sand in front of us. He's assured us that he much prefers fish to mammals who squeal and run when he tries to eat them. I'm not sure I believe him, but now that he's bitten a zombie, I think even the slowest of us can outrun him.

"When?" Wheels says, his greedy eyes on the fish. "We barely had time to think once Emmy took us into battle with another zombie."

Spike rolls her eyes at him, which is a kinder response than I have for the weasel.

"You can go," I say, pointing the way downstream, where we came from.

"Alone? No thanks," he says. "I'd rather be more careful. Why do we have to attack every zombie we come across? Can't we just get back to the camp in one piece?"

"You can," I say, pointing downstream again. If the weasel leaves, I just have to get Diana home, which will be much easier. I may not want to depend on a dog, but dogs are incredibly dependable.

"Can we not fight about this again?" Diana begs.

"Are you going to attack every zombie between us and the camp?" Wheels sputters.

"Zombie is dead," I say, unwilling to give ground to a lesser mammal.

"Bear also dead," Wheels snaps back at me.

I shove the weasel hard. He lands on his back, and I stand over him, my paws fisted. "Bear dead because bear stupid. Not because of me. Not because of Diana. Because bear is too stupid to know zombies." Spike and Diana are watching us tensely, their respective ears flat against their heads.

"Is that enough fish?" the bear asks Diana, lumbering out of the water and breaking the tension for probably the first (and last) time in his life.

She's about to apologize for the tenth time, so I answer for the group. "Yes. Debt paid."

"You're an odd creature," the bear says, staring down at me. "Are you a small bear?"

I don't know whether to be offended or complimented, but Wheels picks himself up from the sand where I shoved him and says, "Ha! I wish. She's a hamster. Way worse."

The way he says it, I am meant to be insulted. I am not. I am much scarier than a bear if this one is any representation of the species.

"Ham-star," the bear says, trying the word out on his clumsy tongue, then sitting down on the beach with a thump. "And you're obviously a weasel."

Wheels nods, reaching for a fish.

"Dog," the bear says, pointing at Diana, and then Spike, "and rabbit."

They nod, and the bear tosses a fish down his gullet. "Never seen such a herd in my life."

"Not a herd," I correct automatically. Herds are too close to families.

"We're from the same camp," Diana says. "We're trying to get back there."

The bear looks confused again, so I take a bite of fish. The sooner we can fuel up and get on our way the better. The first fish is gone, so I start on the next, my stomach satisfied for the first time in a while.

"You travel upriver?" the bear asks, tossing fish bones over his massive shoulder.

"Apparently," mutters the weasel.

"Yes," answers Spike.

"I will come," the bear announces. "More fish upstream, and you can tell me more about these zombies."

We glance at each other. This bear is not going to

have to worry about zombies for much longer. He bit one. Tasted its blood. He is not long for this world.

"Sure," Wheels answers, surprising me.

The bear stands up on all four of his legs and shakes the water from his coat in a spray. "The ham-star will ride on my shoulders and tell me about zombies."

I look up at him and think about how I will look riding a bear into battle. I am not displeased with the mental picture. Who needs a cape?

"I could … ride, and tell you about —" Wheels starts to say.

"Just the ham-star," the bear interrupts before I can object. "I don't trust weasels."

Smarter than I thought.

THE BEAR STARTS OFF at a fast pace, calling questions over his massive shoulder to where I sit, holding on to a large tuft of his hair with my paw. Most of his questions are about how to kill zombies without biting them, which, I have to keep reminding him, won't be a problem for him much longer as he will be dead. But he forgets his impending doom every twenty steps or so, asking questions that are no part of his future.

Diana has fallen behind to make the weasel keep pace. Spike is hopping from left to right ahead of us in a zig-zag, trying to cover all angles. I find myself wishing the cats were with us, because they know more about zombies than any other animal I know. Not so much Ginger, whom I suspect makes up for details he doesn't know with exaggerated anecdotes, but Pickles has gathered a lot of information from her own travels and by listening to the humans at the camp. Hannah learned a lot about the zombies before she met Pickles, and even more about how other animals were fighting the zombies. Even Trip has added to my knowledge about zombies with his adventures rescuing the raccoons from that camp that was experimenting on them.

Am I really missing that misfit band of do-gooder felines? The ones who picked a useless weasel over me?

"And you fight these zombies," the bear presses me.

"I kill zombies," I clarify, glancing at the trees for movement. I thought I saw something in the shadows. More ravens? Damn my poor eyesight!

"Why?"

For a second, I'm confused by the question. There are no other options. This is a kill-or-be-killed moment in time.

"Kills zombies or die," I say finally.

"But that zombie I bit," the bear says, "he wasn't going to kill you."

"Kill someone," I say. "Not me, but you, and some other animal. And another. And bite humans. Make more zombies. Kill all of us."

"So, this odd herd of yours," the bear says, "you search for zombies to kill? That is your purpose?"

"That is my purpose," I reply without hesitation. "The rest are more interested in survival than revenge."

The bear absorbs this, chewing it over slowly like he is eating a fish, and I think he's finally done asking questions, which means I can finally stop talking. I glance back at Diana and notice she's sniffing the air, ignoring the weasel, who is still wasting her time, battering her with questions.

"Who did the zombie kill?"

"Huh?" I say, my eyes on Diana and her brilliantly sensitive nose.

"You said revenge. Who are you avenging?" the bear asks.

I flash to two huge dogs, wrestling with zombies who just hours before had been our pets. Had loved us. And then betrayed us. I've opened my mouth to deny any such connection when streaking out of the darkening forest on our right dart a blur of wolves.

I leap off the bear, yelling for Diana, who starts in shock, her eyes wide and scared. I'm running toward her at top speed, but it's not her the wolves are coming for.

"Come at me, you monsters," yells Spike from the front of our train. I screech to a stop, realizing my mistake. I chose heart over brain again. A dog will be the death of me someday. Today, it might be the death of the Amazonian bunny.

"Spike," squeaks the weasel from where he's dropped to the sandy ground, his paws over his head.

"Don't you dare play dead," I growl over my shoulder.

One of the wolves snaps Spike up in his jaws, but her long, pointy stick keeps him from actually biting her in half. She's cleverly wedged it into place so he can't close his mouth. That and her warrior screams would probably choke him. The bear growls menacingly, but the wolves must smell that he's in no condition to take them on because they just squirt around him and dodge his huge paw as if he's moving in slow motion.

I'm running as fast as I can, Diana at first behind me and then overtaking me as the wolves turn in formation, looping back toward the forest.

I realize we're not going to catch them before they get to the trees, and Diana accelerates, catching up with the slowest of the wolves, snapping at its heels. I have never been more impressed with her. I don't know what she would do if he actually stopped to fight, but maybe she's counting on me to take over the battle. I'd be happy to if they would just slow the heck down. By the Girth of the Capybara, these wolves are fast!

All the canines, the enemies and the ally, disappear into the trees before I even make it to the edge of the forest. I'm still running so hard I can barely breathe, dodging roots, trying to keep Diana's orange coat in my sights, when the ground drops out from under me and I know no more.

CHAPTER SEVEN

"Ham-star." A voice calls me back from unconsciousness.

I blink, pushing my eyelids open with an effort.

The darkness is near complete, with only the light of the moon to show me my new cage.

I struggle to my paws and sniff around. I seem to be in a deep, dark hole. I look up the hole to see the gigantic head of the bear staring down at me.

"Diana?" I growl up at him in question.

He turns his head to talk to someone before turning back to me. "The weasel doesn't know where she or the rabbit are. The canines are long gone."

I punch the earthen wall of my prison and hiss, "Get me out."

The bear leans down into the hole, reaching both his paws in my direction. I jump straight up once, and then again, bouncing off the walls of the hole, and then again and again. I'm not even close to reaching his paws.

The bear sort of collapses at the mouth of the hole, his arms still extended toward me.

"Bear?" I call up.

"Tired," he replies, his tongue lolling out of his mouth. "So hot."

ValHamster is close for this mammal. I look up and into his brown eyes, curious as always about the land of dead warriors.

"I am dying," he says matter-of-factly.

"Yes," I reply, glad he has finally realized this.

The bear gives an infinitesimal nod. "You will go on."

It's a statement, not a question.

"You will save your herd," he says, closing his eyes wearily.

"I will," I vow. This is not the time to correct him.

He stops speaking then, the effort too much for him.

I nod up at his still body. Despite his slow wit, I hope this bear will find his way to ValHamster.

The weasel pokes his head around the body of the bear, and I turn away. There has to be a way to get out of this hole.

"Emmy," calls the weasel, "what do we do?"

I really don't want to answer, so instead I search for sticks I can use to build a ladder. I shove the sticks into the dirt wall and then use a small rock to hammer them in.

"Emmy, answer me," the weasel whines. "Those wolves could come back."

"I hope they come back," I murmur under my breath, giving the sticks another smack. I put my paw on the first one, testing it, and, finding it strong, I climb up. Four sticks up, I am barely a foot off the ground. This is not going to work.

Before I can do more than grimace, though, a ball of fur falls out of the sky and into the hole beside me. It's not the owl I've been hoping for. It's the weasel.

"What are you doing?" I hiss at the ridiculous animal who struggles to sit up.

He finally gains his feet, dusting himself off. "You might not know this about weasels, but we're excellent burrowers."

"I can burrow," I bite back. All hamsters can burrow. I just prefer more aggressive forms of resistance. Like hammering and climbing and fighting.

"Then two of us will get through this faster than one," the weasel replies, testing the walls for the one with the loosest dirt. Deciding on one, he immediately sets to burrowing, his head and arms disappearing quickly into the tunnel he is creating. I stand there, glaring at this annoying creature's tail, considering starting my own tunnel on an opposite wall just so I don't have to work with him side by side. Burrowing with another mammal can be a very intimate experience that I have so far avoided in my life. Imagine it. You're underground, surrounded by darkness and dirt. There's no way to avoid touching. Every scoop of dirt you make has to be pushed aside by another. It's new to me. This dependence.

I've slept in burrows with Pallas, and I've helped design burrows in trees with racoons. But I've never actually burrowed next to another animal.

If I make my own tunnel on the opposite end of this hole, I will be well and truly alone. This weasel is nothing to me. Diana is gone. Spike is gone, maybe even dead. This could be my opportunity. I could leave this weasel behind — strike out on my quest as I planned when I tried to leave the camp.

A wolf howls in the distance, and my decision is made. I scramble into the tunnel behind the weasel. I'm a warrior. The longer I'm down here, the longer Diana is on her own out there, and the more likely Spike's death is. If I can change that fate, I must. Shoulder to shoulder, the weasel and I burrow upwards and sideways in a spiral motion we instinctively know in our bones. We don't need to talk, which is perfect for me, but I have time to think.

The wolves will have a den of some kind where they will gather, and finding it without Diana's nose poses a serious problem.

"I smell air," the weasel announces from in front of me, and his announcement redoubles our efforts. Ten minutes later we are up and out of the tunnel, back on solid ground, amidst the darkness of the trees.

The weasel is panting, but I have no time to get my breath back. I race up the nearest tree, looking for any sign of the wolves. Nothing. Silence, except for the crickets chirping, trying to attract suitable mates and warning each other of the ravens who still circle overhead.

The weasel climbs up beside me, his mouth full of unfortunate bugs.

"What now?" he whispers around the crunching sound.

I do not deign to answer, calculating strategies and discarding them just as quickly. Wishing I could as easily discard this annoying mammal. But when I find Spike, she will ask about him. My answer can't be that I left him behind. That doesn't sound honorable.

"We have to get Diana and Spike back," he whispers emphatically, his paw on my shoulder.

I'm so surprised that I don't bite off his offending paw. This coward? This ... weasel? Is willing to risk his life to save others?

"Dangerous," I whisper, turning to meet the weasel's eyes for the first time in our acquaintance. If he decides to stay behind of his own volition, my warrior's reputation will remain intact. I silently will him to fall back into the treacherous, cowardly ways of his species.

He swallows down the last of the crickets with an audible gulp. "I owe Spike my life. And Diana too. I owe all of you. You don't like me, and that's fine. I've dealt with the prejudice all my life. But I know you're going to save them. I want to help."

Could I have been wrong about this weasel? No one trusts weasels. I learned it at the pet store where I was born. Plus, Vance and Ralph hated weasels more than cats. Or jalapeños. Or thunder. But I've never actually met a weasel myself. Never talked with one. This weasel, though not as brave as the animals I admire, doesn't *seem* evil.

He rubs at his nose, waiting for my answer, but he doesn't drop his eyes from mine.

"We need the ravens," I whisper back finally, looking up at the black bodies cutting through the night, barely discernable against the darkness. "They might know the wolf den."

The weasel nods. "You get them down here, I'll take care of the rest."

I muscle past my distrust, like it's a pile of goofy kittens running through the camp, and put two claws to my mouth, whistling sharply.

The ravens turn immediately toward the sound, so I summon my best Trip-like words. "Ravens, we have business."

CHAPTER EIGHT

Riding ravens is both the best thing I've ever done and the worst. The best because no one needs a cape when riding the dark night winds on the back of an ebony bird. The worst because I don't trust that these fowl animals won't betray us, laughing as they drop us to our deaths.

Normally, that wouldn't bother me in the least. I'd throw myself into this flying adventure like it was the last thing I would ever do. But if I die, who will rescue Diana and Spike? Who will find out if the camp is still there? Or if Pal, Pickles, and all the rest are alive? A glorious death is so final, why doesn't anyone ever talk about that? What is glorious about leaving everyone you love behind to fight without you?

"My den mother used to ride ravens all the time," Wheels says, looking almost comfortable on his large bird, its black feathers glistening against the night sky. If you squint, it's almost like he's riding the wind itself.

"What happened to her?"

The weasel shakes his head. "I don't know. We were attacked by zombies, and we ran in all directions. Spike and her pet saved me, but we never found anyone else. I made Spike wait to see if anyone would return to the burrow, but no one did."

His story sounds very like Trip's. We are all orphans in this new zombie-filled world.

"My den mother would trade for food, shiny things we found, all kinds of stuff. The weasels on my mom's side of the family are well-known fliers."

I find I have no answer for this revelation. I want to doubt him because I doubt anything that comes out of a weasel's mouth, but here we are, riding the winged beasts. Some of his story must be true.

"A whole box of cat fur," the raven I am riding reminds me with a caw. He's making a real effort to communicate, because normally, I wouldn't understand a word he says.

"A whole box. Just find the big gray cat named Wally," I promise again. The things these scavengers treasure are as random as their loyalty. Much like the bargains I've witnessed Trip negotiate, the ravens argued amongst themselves about the trade. I had to push down my impatience, my fear over what was happening to

Diana and Spike, waiting for the stupid birds to finally land on a price we could deliver. Wheels came up with the idea. A box of cat fur, to be delivered by the felines back at our camp. I had disagreements with the cats, but they were honorable mammals. They would deliver on our promise, and by involving Wally, who shared my distrust of, well, everything, these birds would be hard-pressed to steal more than they were promised. And if the camp were destroyed, well, these fell beasts would no doubt seek us out to renegotiate the bargain. And I would have more information about The Menagerie.

"The den," the raven says, slightly out of breath. I hoped they would direct us. Who knew they could carry us? The weasel. He knew and made the trade. I squint down at the cave as the raven makes a tight circle, his peer following us.

"Land there," I say, pointing at a copse of trees to the left of the cave. My eyes may not be the best in the animal kingdom, but I'm practiced at picking out strategic attack points. I leap off the raven before he even lands on the branch, my eyes searching everywhere for Diana's bright orange coat. I squint at the cave, my eyes shooting lasers of intimidation.

"What are you doing?"

I ignore the weasel's disrespectful question, and the ravens take off, flying after their promised box of cat fur.

I keep one ear trained on the skies in case they turn back and betray us.

My poor eyesight means that I hear Spike before I see her. Wheels bursts into sniveling tears of relief behind me on the branch. I give him a hard poke, and then run down along the branch toward Spike's echoing voice. She sounds like she's threatening someone.

"Back," she hisses, a lit branch in her paws. She's inside the cave, but just barely, her back to one of the rocky walls. The wolves are panting and growling within feet of her location. Diana is nowhere to be seen, but she had the last match in her collar. Surely that's how Spike got that burning branch.

"What do we do? What do we do?" Wheels whispers from my left, the tears in his voice still audible.

"How many wolves do you count?" I hiss at the weasel.

"Five," he blubbers.

I feel the warrior's cloak drop over my shoulders, the battle lust rising. Five wolves. I could take at least three of them. Maybe all five with Spike's help.

I grab a branch next to me, wresting it free of the tree and handing it to Wheels. "Defend Spike. Watch for Diana. Good hunting."

The weasel looks shocked, and I'm not sure if it's the cowardice bubbling back up or if he's surprised that I included him in my attack plan.

I don't stick around to figure it out. I leap from my

position with a bellow as loud as a lion on the savannah in those TV documentaries my pet sometimes watched. The wolves jump apart, and I hit the ground at a roll. I grab a small branch in my teeth and run straight to Spike's side to light my own stick on hers.

"Took you long enough."

"Fell in a hole."

"Where's Wheels?"

I point at the tree where I left the weasel, expecting him to be standing there, still holding the branch in his shaking paw. But I can't see him from this distance. Then the wolves close back around us, and I bare my teeth.

"There are two now," says one of the wolves, licking her lips.

"All the better," says her straggly-looking peer.

"That's what you think," I hiss, diving under the nearest wolf and poking the lit branch up at his underside. I roll left, careful not to lose my weapon as the wolf tears off into the underbrush, howling. I don't see the paw that comes swiping from behind me, knocking me into the side of the cave wall. I pick myself up, trying to get my eyes to refocus. Spike is jumping around so fast she's a blur of long ears, sparks, and fuzzy tail. I hear the snap of jaws too close to my foot and leap backwards, whirling like a dervish to face my next opponent. Only he's not facing me. He's looking back at the trees, his nose in the air. Actually, all the wolves are looking at the darkened forest, sniffing, paying no attention to the mammals with fire sticks. Their mistake. I race from wolf to wolf, stabbing painful parts of their anatomy and lighting tails on fire, narrowly missing the pair of zombies who stomp their way out of the treeline.

The wolves (lit and unlit) tear away, yipping and yapping their fear into the night, but I'm watching for what's behind the zombies — the animal who has driven these zombies into our midst. This battle isn't over. Sure enough, a once bright-orange mammal barks from the edge of the forest, signaling her strategy.

"Diana!" I say, dodging a clumsy attempt from the skinny zombie to grab me and running up its pant leg. Spike has already climbed her zombie, bouncing from shoulder to shoulder lighting the undead attacker, and then jumping to the nearest tree branch, out of the flaming zombie's reach.

The zombies are on fire, waving at the air with flaming arms.

"Emmy," Diana calls, her coat covered in dirt and leaves and who knows what else, nearly unrecognizable but for her beautiful fox face. "Over here!"

"Zombies," I say, nodding at Diana with an appreciative grin. "Good weapons."

She's panting, tired from her efforts of rounding up zombies and luring them here, but she returns my grin. "Weaponized zombies, patent pending."

The zombies are basically dealt with, even if they don't know it, as their limbs crumble to ash and they sink to the forest floor. I wait until the twitching stops and then stamp them a bit to make sure. Two guaranteed ways to get rid of zombies — remove their heads or burn them to ash.

"Diana?" Spike says, her voice full of wonder. "You came back for me?"

"Of course I did, silly," she says, laughing.

"I lost sight of you when we got to the cave," Spike says, "after you threw me the last match."

"I couldn't smell Emmy anymore," Diana says, "but I smelled the zombies and thought the wolves might take them more seriously than a corgi and a rabbit with a bit of fire."

"Your dog is not normal," Spike says to me, throwing her arms around the corgi. "She's amazing."

Pride wells up in me before I can stop it. When my anger and feelings of vengeance recede, all kinds of other emotions show up. I hate that. Next, you'll find me blubbering about the healing power of sharing like a racoon.

Spike brushes some soot off Diana's coat with her fluffy tail before asking me again, "Now, where is Wheels?"

I point at the branch again, leading Spike and Diana to the tree where I left the crying mammal. Along the way I explain about the death of the bear and the hole I had to dig my way out of.

"You burrowed out?" Spike asked.

I know I should say that "we" burrowed our way out of the hole, but I don't. It feels weird to admit aloud that I needed anyone's help. Especially a weasel's help. Which, of course, I didn't.

Diana is the first to react to the smell. "Whoa, what is that? It's horrible."

The stink washes over us, and I recognize it immediately, though Spike says it aloud. "It's Wheels. He must have …"

She doesn't get the chance to finish that sentence because suddenly I notice the eyes all around us, and I jump in front of her, teeth bared. They're not wolves. They're too low to the ground. And they're not growling. Their teeth are chattering in unison. Turns out that's worse.

CHAPTER NINE

Have you ever seen a human wig? Terrifying things. Bodiless beings of hair and net that seem to levitate on the head of the humans who wear them. My pet's father wore one, and he would leave it on the counter in the human litter box overnight to stoke my nightmares. Imagine a long-haired blond wig stepping out of the shadows of the forest. But this wig has pink eyes. And his equally hairy friends are carrying what look like the lids of cat food tins, decorated with symbols I don't recognize.

He casts his weird pink eyes over us, from the dirtiest corgi you've ever seen to a small hissing rabbit pointing a still-hot stick at them with visceral malice to me, the most obvious threat of the bunch.

"I am Rumiñawi," the long-haired wig says, his accent exaggerated, like a really bad impression of a Latin accent that you only ever hear on late-night TV. "You have trespassed into our territory and must leave."

"Your territory?" Spike hisses at the mammal.

The talking wig ignores her, his eyes locked on mine, which I assume is in deference to my intimidating presence. "You will escort your pack out of the area immediately and not return."

"Hey, look, we didn't mean to … trespass on anything, Ruminini … Ruminwawi … Mr. Guinea Pig," Diana says, ever the peacekeeper. "We're just trying to get home."

Again, the wig/guinea pig ignores her words, waiting for me to answer. I run my eyes over the throng of armed guinea pigs, the way their paws hold their tin shields. This is a trained squadron of zombie fighters. How cool is that? Maybe they're looking for another warrior.

"We're not going anywhere. We need to find our …" I hesitate here, because exactly what *is* Wheels now? He's not the entirely useless weasel I assumed him to be. He got us here on the backs of ravens, no less. He helped dig me out of a hole. The warrior part of me takes up the biggest sword available to battle back from these admissions in my head, pointing out that I could have accomplished both those heroic acts on my own. But if they were indeed heroic acts, then wasn't the weasel at least a little heroic?

"Our friend," Diana inserts helpfully. "He's a weasel.

Maybe you've seen him? He's lanky, with a light brown coat, and he rubs his nose a lot when he's thinking."

"The weasel is our prisoner," Rumiñawi says. "You will go, and be thankful we saved you from his deceptive claws."

Instead of being pleased that these guinea pigs know about the evil nature of weasels, I feel a spark of worry about Wheels rise in my chest like a flaming arrow shot into the sky. Am I starting to care what happens to the weasel that made me leave my home? What is wrong with me?

"I'm not leaving without Wheels ..." Spike starts to say, shoving her way in front of me.

She's interrupted by a wolf howl that freezes all conversation.

"They're coming back this way," Diana announces, sniffing the air, her ears flattening against her head. "More of them. Lots more."

Rumiñawi signals with a flick of his mane, and half his troop scampers left into the shadowy forest.

Spike is undecided on who to face first, the remaining guinea pigs or the imminently arriving wolves. She faces the forest, then whips around to face Rumiñawi and then back again, her cotton tail quivering in anticipation of a battle. I feel my own blood rising. I'm not abandoning Spike to this fight, and right or wrong, she's not leaving without the weasel. Warriors don't run from combat, and in this moment, I am blessed with the potential of two glorious battles. Besides, this particular weasel may have earned enough of my respect that I won't leave him behind. He hasn't changed my mind about weasels as a species, but he may have been improved by his time with Spike, becoming a less cowardly version of the animal he was. That transformation should be rewarded. I will deliver him to The Menagerie and let them continue his education.

"Fight us and the wolves," I say to Rumiñawi, "or we fight the wolves with you. Either way, we're not leaving without the weasel."

Rumiñawi flicks his other cowlick, prompting the rest of his troop to turn in formation. "Your loyalty is misplaced. The weasel will have a chance to defend himself for his trespass, but we have not the time to discuss it here. Come with us."

I deflate a little. I was looking forward to testing my mettle against these furry rodents.

Diana releases her breath, happy to pick the unknown safety of guinea pigs over the known danger of a wolf pack we've already ticked off. She follows them into the darkness, as does Spike. I knew Spike would follow, if only to gain entrance to their territory and survey for signs of the weasel. I scowl into the forest, daring a lone wolf to dart out and try to stop us from this escape, but there's not a canine muzzle to be seen. I take my time stamping out the last of the smoldering zombie bodies and then follow Diana and Spike.

The guinea pigs lead the way into a dense, thorny bush, and Diana stops. "Um ... I don't think I'll fit through there ..." she says, pointing her black nose at the space between thorns that a guinea pig just disappeared through.

Rumi turns his pink eyes toward the sky, and I follow his gaze to the ropes wrapped around a branch. Like magic, a three-foot piece of the thorny bush suddenly lifts off the forest floor. Diana looks to me, and I nod, so she scoots down and underneath the raised thorn gate, her white underside sliding against the forest floor. I follow her to the next gate, which goes through the same process, the gate behind us lowering as this one is raised. Then we're in the belly of the beast, a large, open space with thorny bush above and all around us. I stare up at the night sky through the canopy of thorns and wonder if this is a human-built contraption. Was the center cleared out for some purpose evident only to humans? Trip would know. As a city raccoon, born and bred, his relationship with humans and all their engineering feats is a source of unrelenting fascination for the members of The Menagerie. He loves tunnels and trains and bridges and fidget spinners. Even more than that, he loves to tell stories about them. I smile that I will have a story to tell him when we get back home and then remember that it's not my home anymore. Diana will have to tell him this story instead of me.

Tiny fires are lit around the edges of this camp, with small groups of guinea pigs gathered around them, eating or sleeping. The number of colors the guinea pigs exhibit reminds me of my pet store origins. Guinea pigs were very popular with humans, as I recall, in cages next to mine. I never understood their appeal, but who knew they could fight? Maybe the long-haired ones are the warriors and the short-haired ones are the gatherers.

"You admire them," Diana whispers from beside me.

I nod without even thinking about it. This is a brilliantly designed fortress. "I wonder how many zombies they have killed," I say aloud. I wonder to myself if it's as many as I have. Doubt it.

Diana looks sad at my approval of this stronghold, but the truth is, our camp with the humans has too many amenities. It was built for comfort as much as it was built for defense. The point of a home base is to have a safe space to regroup and then return to the fight. It is not for comfort and family. That was the problem with our house in our neighborhood. The doors barely withstood the zombies when they attacked. Which is how my pets fell. Which is how my dogs fell. Which is why I burned the entire neighborhood to ash. Maybe if our camp were less comfortable, random mammals wouldn't show up looking for a spot in The Menagerie. These guinea pigs seem to understand that.

A dark hole in the middle of the cleared space draws my attention, but before I can investigate, we hear the arrival of the wolves around us.

The canines know exactly where we are, and we can hear their low growls from all around. They're close enough that I can smell the singed fur. I grin a wicked grin. Yes, they brought the rest of their pack, but the ones we defeated will smell like nasty burned fur for weeks. I hope the guinea pigs notice. Warriors relish recognition from like-minded heroes.

Diana sticks herself to my side like a magnet on a fridge, her ears flicking left and right.

"Are we sure they can't get in?" she whispers out of the side of her mouth.

I glare at the yellow wolf eye I can see through the many layers of thorn bush, wishing they would try. "This isn't the first time these guinea pigs have gone to war."

Maybe I will wait till these animals fall asleep and then take on the wolves myself. That would impress these rodents!

"It is not," Rumi agrees from one of the fires, where he has spread out a small feast. I try not to stare at the celery stick he's chewing, but I haven't seen or tasted a celery stick in a very long time. I wonder where he got it from. It's not a vegetable our humans seem committed

to growing or providing to the mammals of our compound. I must be doing a bad job of disguising my envy,
because he picks up another bright green celery stick
from behind him and extends it my way. It's gone in
seconds. Delicious. This camp is looking more and more
appealing. Rumi smiles and waves a carrot at Spike, who
is walking the perimeter glaring at the wolves she can
hear but not fight. "Worry not, rabbit. They cannot get
in. Many have tried. None have succeeded."

Diana sits down near the fire close to me, accepting
the food being offered to her by other guinea pigs of the
troop. I know she prefers fish or meat when she can get
it, but she takes a hesitant bite of a mushroom. She can't
seem to relax with the growling sounds, and I assume
that she actually understands some of what the wolves
are hissing at us, and it can't be good. I'm guessing it
involves comparisons between us and litter paper.

I take Rumi at his word that we are safe within these
thorns. I'm on my third celery stick before Spike finally
sits down and glares at me for my mealtime betrayal. I
swallow down my food before nudging the carrot in
her direction. I know she's worried about the weasel,
but as always, I'm thinking about the next fight, and
that requires fuel. I try to communicate this through
my whiskers, but either I fail or Spike doesn't care for
my rationalizations.

"You will stay here tonight," Rumi says, wiping his

paws on his wig of hair, twirling a strand into a pompadour. "You will be safe."

Spike looks like she wants to throw the carrot at the walking blond wig like a dart, but Diana speaks before she can do it. "Thank you, Mr. Guinea Pig. We appreciate the safety of your camp. And the food."

"What about Wheels?" Spike demands.

"I told you, the weasel will have a chance to defend himself," Rumi repeats, his long fur rippling. "I'll speak no more on the matter."

If Spike's ears got any more stiff, she would be able to row a boat with them. Through a tsunami.

"Tomorrow," he says, pausing to look each of us in the eyes one after the other, "you leave. Before the sun rises. You will be on your way and never return."

Spike just clenches her jaw, which makes her two front teeth jut out even further. Diana and I nod sagely because there really is no choice with wolves growling all around us and a legion of armed guinea pigs with us, surrounded by a thorny bush that is as much a prison as it is a castle. Spike and I could maybe squeeze our way through the thorns to take on the wolves, but not Diana. And what about Wheels? No, the fight outside the thorned bush can wait while we locate the weasel. It's all about priorities. Rumi flicks his hair again, and all the guinea pigs walk to another fire pit, leaving this one to us.

"We need to find Wheels now," Spike whispers, gripping the carrot so tightly it snaps in her paws.

Diana sniffs the air. "He's here for sure, but … he's not alone."

"What do you mean?" I whisper, chewing on a kernel of corn and trying to look like a good guest and, potentially, a good ally. "Another weasel?"

Diana shakes her head immediately. "Not another weasel."

"Eat," I suggest, pushing both broken pieces of carrot at the rabbit. "Keep your strength up. Once camp has settled for the night, we free the weasel."

"You promise?" Spike asks, the anger in her eyes receding slightly, her ears relaxing out of their rigid stance. I realize that she really thought she was alone in this rescue. I can't blame her. I haven't kept my dislike of weasels to myself.

"Promise," I say, realizing that sometimes, you really do need to say things out loud. And I mean it. Even if I decide to stay with these warrior guinea pigs for a few battles, it's not a home, and it's no place for a non-combatant like the weasel. He would need to leave, ideally on his own paws.

Despite her worries, Spike gobbles down enough food for a bear and then, leaning against Diana, who has splooted right in front of the food, falls asleep almost mid-chew.

I wait, not really sleeping, but not moving either, my paws pulled underneath me, right up next to Diana's left ear. The guinea pigs are basically dormant, in piles around their extinguished fire pits. The chittering finally transitions to snoring, and I can't hear the wolves anymore either. I look up through the thorns, catching sight of blurs of flying creatures, wondering if Pal would be able to see us in here. Probably not. I stare skywards anyway.

CHAPTER TEN

The cool air of twilight seeps into the thorny camp before I feel comfortable investigating.

"It's time," I whisper directly into Diana's ear. She flicks it at me like I'm a gnat, so I risk getting up and slide over to Spike.

She senses me and opens one eye. "Now?"

"Now," I agree, leading the way to the hole in the center of this fortification.

We carefully pad our way to the edge of the hole and look down to see two mammals positioned as far away from each other as physically possible.

"Wheels," Spike hisses, recognizing the weasel in the darkness right away. I'm squinting at the other animal, trying to recognize it and feeling like I do.

It picks its head up, and two big glowing eyes stare up at me, filled with such sadness that they make me take a step away from the hole.

"We have to get him out," Spike whispers at me. My eyes are still locked on the unfortunate second animal, my brain fighting with my heart.

Wheels doesn't respond to Spike's repeated hisses, but the young animal looks from Wheels to us and back again before whispering in a soft voice, "Do you want me to try and wake him?"

Spike looks horrified at the idea and hisses back, "Stay away from him, you … you dog!"

He's a dog, yes, but even more … I think he's a very young Great Dane. I can tell by his long, rectangular head and square jaw. He's young enough that he and the weasel are about the same size.

The puppy seems to be too used to the angry voice directed his way and turns away from us, burying his face under his long tail without another sound. I remember stories I have overheard from Hannah about her experiences before she met Pickles. When she talked about the abuse she suffered at the paws of cruel, bullying cats, she would seem to contract into herself, becoming a smaller version of her usually tall, lithe body. This pup's reaction reminds me of that physical reaction. Some animals get smaller and talk more when confronted with trauma, and some animals get bigger and quieter. I went the second way. I don't know why, but I can see how it happens.

"Emmy," Spike says, actually poking me in the shoulder

to get me to look her way. "Are you listening to me? We have to get Wheels out of there."

"Both of them," I hear myself saying, my voice gluey with emotions.

Spike is the one to stare at me now. "Both of them? Why? No, the dog … we don't want to have some yappy puppy dog following us around."

"Why not?"

"Look, I know how you feel about Diana, and … she's a special case," Spike admits, glancing back at the sleeping corgi, "but I'm telling you, she's not a normal dog. She doesn't bite you or chase you or bark like she's nuts and attract zombies. But this puppy … we just can't take a chance. They can't be trusted," Spike says.

"Like weasels?"

"No! Not like weasels," Spike answers angrily. "You've got things all backwards. And I don't have time to explain it again. You stay here. I'm going to grab some food for Wheels. Be ready."

With that, she slides back to Diana and the pile of food.

I glance around at the piles of sleeping guinea pigs. They may be fighters, but these are not mammals of honor. They threw a defenseless weasel and a puppy in a hole. I will not fight alongside them. I crouch down so that I'm lying right beside the hole, as if I've rolled here in a fitful sleep.

"Hey," I whisper down at the pup.

He tries to ignore me, but I know that he is curious. Finally, he looks back up at me from under his tail.

"Are you going to yell at me too?"

"Never," I promise, and I mean it. Wow, it's hard looking him in the face like this. "I'm Emmy. And that weasel over there — his name is Wheels."

I wait, and finally, the pup says, "I'm Chewie."

"Chewie," I repeat, testing out. "I like it. Did you pick it?"

The puppy looks confused by the question. "No. My pets named me just before they ran away from the zombies. I only knew them for a few days. They left me behind."

My heart thuds at that sad betrayal. It's time for both of us to change tactics: this puppy will have to regain his confidence, and I will have to relocate my words to help him get there. "How did you get here? In this hole?" I ask.

Chewie gives his head a shake before answering. "I kept getting chased by zombies, by big cats, by mean rats … no one had time for me. Eventually, I left the rows of houses and made it down to a ravine. I fell asleep one night under a bush, and when I woke up I was surrounded by these scary hairy animals. They put me down here. I can't really climb out on my own."

He turns his face to his lower quarters, and I notice that yes, he has only one hind leg. As a pup, he probably hasn't had time to adjust to his three-legged reality, but I have met other mammals with missing limbs who more than kept up with their peers. An unfriendly goat who lives at the camp springs to mind. When we got these two out of this situation, I would have to introduce them.

"If you want, you could come with us," I offer.

"Come with you?" he asks, sitting up a bit. "How? Where?"

"Somewhere better than this hole for sure," I promise. "Somewhere with kind, clever animals, and caring pets, and enough food."

"You come from a place like that?" Chewie asks, wonder making his voice wispy. "And I could really come with you?"

"Really," I say, fighting the urge to describe my reasons for leaving. They seem oddly unimportant now when weighed against the good things about The Menagerie that I want Chewie to experience.

I turn my eyes to the immobile lump at the other end of the hole.

"He's knocked out," Chewie says, following my gaze. "Landed on his head when the guinea pigs threw him down here. He's not the most graceful animal."

To my surprise, I find myself defending Wheels. "He was thrown in a hole," I growl. "Grace has nothing to do with it." Plus, I think, he's probably playing dead. It's his signature move. Based on how the guinea pigs seem to feel about weasels, it might have saved his life this time.

Chewie's brown eyes get wider, and I realize that growl betrayed my anger, but it wasn't directed at him. It was for his captors. "I'm going to get you both out of there," I promise him, purposefully softening my tone for maybe the second time in my life.

That's, of course, when Spike shuffles back to my side, her arms laden with vegetables for the weasel. "Why are you talking to that dog?"

"His name is Chewie, and we're getting him out of that hole," I say, angry at Spike for the first time since we fought a zombie and fell off a cliff together.

Spike's eyes narrow to slits. "Fine. But he's your problem."

"Who's your problem?" Diana asks sleepily, wandering over to where we sit by the hole. "Hey, Wheels! You found him. And who is this sweet pup?"

Chewie stands up excitedly, barking up at Diana. "Hi! I'm Chewie!"

"Shhh!" I say, trying to calm the pup down so he doesn't wake up the guinea pigs.

"See!" hisses Spike, waving her paws at the puppy. "Dogs are loud!"

Diana drops to her belly and sticks her snout into the hole as far down as she can. "Hi, Chewie, aren't you a darling? We have to be quiet. Can you hear me if I whisper? I'm Diana."

Chewie looks so happy to see another dog I think he's going to wag his tail right off. Diana's entire back end is dancing as well. Like I said, dogs have two moods: crazy happy and wretchedly sad. I never want to see Chewie wretchedly sad again. It might break my heart.

"What are you doing down there with Wheels?" Diana asks, interrupting my thought.

"We're going to fight," Chewie says, his tongue lolling out of his mouth. "Do you know any other dogs, Diana?"

"Wait, you're going to what?" Spike interrupts.

"Fight! The guinea pigs feed the winner," Chewie explains. "I had to learn to fight other animals, but I've gotten pretty good. And I'm so very hungry. Diana is a nice name. Where's your tail?"

"I … my tail?" Diana answers, looking back up at us in confusion and growing horror at Chewie's words.

"Rumi said there would be an opportunity for Wheels to defend himself," I say, understanding the dilemma immediately.

"You know Wheels can't defend himself against a dog," Spike says, glaring down at Chewie. "He's not a fighter."

"He won't have to be," I say, the words shocking me as they come out of my mouth. Am I actually suggesting *not* fighting our way out of a situation? I've spent too much time with strategically minded war-avoiding felines like Pickles and Wally. But I have an idea that I think they would be proud of. "You don't really want to hurt Wheels, do you, Chewie?"

"Of course not," Chewie says, his eyes going back and forth between me and Diana.

"You've got an idea," Diana says to me.

"I do, but I need everyone to trust me," I say, looking up to watch Rumi emerge from his sleeping place, followed by a cadre of his guinea pigs. "Especially you, Chewie. Do you want to come with us?"

Chewie nods his head so hard his eyes cross.

Spike looks down into the hole, her whole body vibrating with doubt. The puppy glances away from her heated gaze.

"I trust you, Emmy," Spike says to me, her eyes still on the puppy. "If you promise to get Wheels out of there, I'll follow your lead."

"Chewie, you have to do what Emmy says," Diana says, using her newfound influence over the younger dog. "No matter how weird it sounds."

Chewie stares up at her and nods, his eyes wide. "I will. I promise. You won't leave me?"

"Never," Diana whispers down at him. "We never leave family behind."

I feel a smile tugging at my mouth for the first time in a long time, but there is a new battle to fight, and it won't involve my claws or Diana's wiles.

"Strangers," Rumi says as I approach him, "the sun will be up soon. I think it is time you kept your word and left this place."

"We will be on our way," I agree. "Heading directly west, the way we came, right, Spike?"

"Riiight," Spike says, sounding unconvincing to my ear.

"West, straight through the gate and onwards," Diana says much more believably, and then barks a few times for emphasis, getting Chewie's attention. I hope he understood.

Rumi nods in satisfaction, flicking his hair at his underlings. The signal prompts a bunch of guinea pigs to run toward the ropes that will raise the thorn door.

"But we need to bury our friend first," I say.

Rumi tilts his pompadour at me in confusion. "Bury your friend?" He looks at Spike and then at Diana.

"Our friend Wheels. He died during the night. He was very weak," I say, pointing at the hole, "with Crowvid-19."

The guinea pigs are all ears now, even the ones holding the ropes.

"Crowvid-19?" Rumi repeats at me.

"He caught it from riding crows," I explain, shaking my head. "A common sickness amongst those fowl creatures. And weasels, well, they aren't the most careful mammals."

"When you came upon us, we knew he was dying. We were getting ready to cremate him," Diana says, catching on to my strategy. "That's why we had the fire."

The guinea pigs around us are now looking at each other, whispering amongst themselves.

"The wolves interrupted us," Spike says, nodding. "Now we have no fire, but we can still bury our friend. It's the least we can do."

"We wouldn't want anyone else to get sick," I say, planting my final seed.

The guinea pigs finally break ranks and scamper around looking for water to cleanse themselves of this disease they've brought into their camp. Now it's like someone dropped two dozen wigs on the floor and they are all playing the floor is lava.

"He is not dead," Rumi says, though his hair starts to look a little limp as he says these words. He pads over to the hole behind us, dodging frantic guinea pigs, and calls down, "You, dog, poke him."

Chewie looks up at Diana, who gives an infinitesimal nod, and then the pup pokes the weasel. He pokes him again. He finally rolls him over so that Wheels is lying face down in the hole. That is professional-level playing dead he's doing down there. At least I hope he's playing dead.

Rumi backs up in horror, trips over a pure white wig/ guinea pig, and says, "We will fill in the hole. Get the dog out ... we will get dirt and ..."

"Oh no, the dog is infected too now," I say, shaking

my head sadly at the puppy in the hole. "He will be gone soon. You need to bury him too. Just to be safe."

I don't know Chewie, but any animal would be freaking out at this suggestion. He stares up at us, his eyes begging to be saved. But he says nothing. He doesn't even whine like I'm sure he wants to. Dogs are loyal to the very end.

"Do it. Listen to the hamster," Rumi commands from his prostrate position, giving in to verbal commands over his limp and unresponsive hair. "Bury them in dirt. Do it now."

"Well, if you've got this, we will be on our way," I say, walking away from the hole. "If you could open these gates?"

"Yes, begone," Rumi says, totally distracted at this point, his exaggerated accent gone. "Our kindness has been answered with disease. We will never have dealings outside of our own kind again. It's not safe. And I advise you to never set paw in our territory again."

"Like we asked to be jumped in the forest," Spike says under her breath, but none of the guinea pigs are paying attention. They're too freaked out.

Somehow, Rumi gets the guinea pigs organized enough to pull the ropes that will release us back into the forest.

"Go," I say to Diana as soon as the gate is raised high enough, and then I follow her out.

"West?" she asks.

"West," I agree.

"What's west?" Spike whispers, following us.

We get behind a bush directly west of the gate, and I start digging immediately. "Help me!"

Spike and Diana leap into action, digging beside me, following my lead. We go down at an angle, with no spiral at all, and we keep going and going until the sun is well above the horizon. I imagine that my paws are the giant claws of a panther and, as I push the dirt behind me, that my hind paws have the power of a full-grown kangaroo. I dig. I don't stop for breath or rest, but my brain is buzzing. I start to think this plan was too complex for a young puppy and a terrified weasel. I start to wonder if I've lost another dog who looked at me with trust in his eyes.

That's when a snout I recognize pushes its way out of the dirt in front of us.

"Wheels," breathes Spike, digging more frantically.

"Spike! Thank the Wolverine," Wheels says weakly as soon as his entire head is out. "I didn't know where or when it would be safe to come up. I just heard Emmy say to aim the tunnel west."

We pull Wheels out of the tunnel and then, with his help, dig out Chewie, who was right behind him, learning to dig beside the weasel as they escaped their grave.

"Did I do it right?" Chewie gasps as soon as he is free. "Mr. Wheels?"

"You did it perfectly," Wheels says, wrapping his scrawny arms around the shaking puppy. "We'll make a burrowing animal out of you yet."

CHAPTER ELEVEN

I make the tired animals travel far beyond the guinea pigs' territory before we stop for a rest. Back beside the river, we make camp in the wide open, the rope bridge within our sight, recognizable in the distance. Well, to be honest, a blur between two cliffs for me, but confirmed by the weasel's next words.

"I see the bridge," Wheels says, pointing and then yawning loudly. He falls to his knees and then onto his back, spread-eagled in the sand.

"Come on, Chewie, let's clean you up," Diana suggests, coaxing the young pup into the shallows to wash off the dirt and grime of the tunnel.

He's so sleepy that he follows her into the water without a word of protest.

"He's only a few months old," I say to no one in particular. Vance and Ralph were full-grown dogs by the time I arrived at the house, but I think they would have fallen in love with Chewie. They were big softies at heart.

Spike is lying next to Wheels, soaking up the sun on the beach, regaining her strength, but she turns her head my way. "You were right about him, Emmy. We were right to save him. He's just a baby. I'm starting to change my mind about dogs. Maybe they're not all bad."

I nod, turning my gaze away from the dogs and swallowing my regrets. Heroes don't lie. "You … were right too."

"I think she's talking about me," Wheels says, his eyes closed but his grin wide. He's surprisingly at ease for someone who just escaped certain death by a colony of human wigs.

"I am," I confirm. "Wheels showed courage. He's not a fighter. But he has honor."

Wheels smiles wider, his eyes still closed. "The hamster likes me, Spike."

Spike smiles back. "I told you I'd find us a new home, Wheels."

I feel the familiar worries creep back in at the word *home*. Here is another mammal I could call a friend. Another friend to lose to the zombies. Chewie drags himself out of the shallows to collapse next to Wheels. Another dog whose loyalty and love I will never be able to repay.

"Hey, can we talk?" Diana asks, calling me out of the

downward spiral my thoughts are taking me in.

I follow the corgi out of earshot of the other mammals.

"I can do this, you know," she says, shaking herself off a bit before sitting down in the sand. She's back to her bright orange self, the dirt and soot gone, her white paws pristine once more.

I tilt my head. What is she talking about?

"I can get us to the rope bridge," she says, pointing her nose at our goal, "and according to Wheels and what he remembers of that map, it's very close to our camp. Barely an hour's walk."

I glance at the bridge. Is she saying what I think she's saying?

"You got us here. I can take them the rest of the way, and you can ...," she trails off here, "go off on your own. That's what you wanted, right? I stopped you from leaving that night, and then the zombie and the cliff ..."

I nod immediately. Of course that's what I want.

"You're not worried about Wheels anymore, are you?"

"No," I reply, feeling a swirl of emotions that make it hard to answer her questions.

"Good. Then I can do this, Emmy," Diana says, "and you can go on with your mission."

On my own. Yes. I look at the puppy lying next to the weasel and the rabbit. It's better this way. Probably.

"I will get you to the rope bridge," I say to Diana, not looking her in the eye, "and then I will go on my mission."

"Warriors are generous," Diana answers with a smile I can hear in her voice. "Thank you, Emmy."

We give the rest of the mammals an hour to rest, and I am left to my own thoughts. In a small circle, they share the battle stories that got them to this point. The weasel recounts our adventure riding ravens through the dark night sky. The rabbit describes getting free of the wolf's jaws and setting the wolves against each other until Diana arrived bearing the match. The pup listens agape to Diana's decision to leave Spike with the fire and the wolves to find zombies. Then he retells his story of being captured by the guinea pigs and being forced to fight for his food. I hear all this from a small burrow in a tree, out of sight of them all. I need to think, but all I can hear are their voices and their shared pride. They're leaving out important points of valor, and I have to fight the urge to leap out and join them with corrections. Sharing is for family. It's loud and emotional and leads to feelings. If you don't feel togetherness, you can't feel loss. You can't be betrayed. Anger is so much easier.

At least when I am alone I will be rid of this constant chatter. I will be able to think. To focus on my mission of ridding this world of zombies. They're whispering now, and I can't hear their words. Which is better, of course. Gives me more time to plan my strategy. My battle plan. I think back to my dreams of zombie elimination and my magnificent cape. Of ValHamster and how I will earn my place there. For some reason, they're harder to call to mind.

"Emmy," a voice calls, "we're ready when you are."

We set out again, this time led by the rabbit, followed by the weasel, then the dogs, and I bring up the rear. Spike is in high spirits, mimicking Rumi and his hair-based communication style, making Wheels laugh. Wheels is now carrying a stick to match Spike's, though he's using it as a walking staff, blunting the sharpened end. The puppy is having trouble keeping up with the pace the rabbit has set and drops behind.

"I need to talk to Spike," Diana says. "Emmy, can you walk with Chewie?"

I nod at her, and she springs ahead to walk between Spike and Wheels. Whatever she's saying to them, they're listening intently, and Spike's cotton tail is stock still, indicating it's serious stuff.

"Diana is amazing," the puppy says, drawing me out of my observations. His tongue is lolling out of his mouth. "Are all dogs like her?"

"She's the first other dog you've met?" I ask, watching Wheels' tail swish from side to side like he's disagreeing with Diana.

"I think so," Chewie answers. "I don't remember much before my pets rescued me. I think I might have been an only pup. I don't remember a litter of brothers or sisters. Or even my mother."

"So, you weren't from a store with other animals?"

"What's a store?" Chewie asks.

I wonder if he was left somewhere as the runt of the litter and shake my head at the cruelty of humans. "Diana is a fine dog. But I told you, where you're going, there are many fine animals."

"Diana says she lives in a camp with lots of human pets," Chewie says, his tail smacking me in his excitement. I remember that too. Vance was much larger than Chewie, and when he got excited, I had to dodge getting swatted off a table by that tail. I would use it to practice my self-defense techniques, jumping over the tail, ducking under it. Vance and Ralph found it hilarious. Their laughter was contagious. When was the last time I laughed like that?

Instead, I nod at this miniature version of my lost first friends, swallowing that memory with less pain than before.

"And she says she lives with lots of cats and a raccoon and an owl," Chewie continues, frowning a bit. "I'm not sure what a raccoon is, but I'm pretty sure I've seen an owl in the ravine. They are scary and loud."

"Our owl isn't scary or loud," I say, squinting into

the distance. Did thinking of Pal make him appear? My heart leaps with hope. Is that an owl on the other side of the rope bridge? My eyesight isn't great, but the brown blur seems to be moving like my friend. That sort of jerky up-and-down motion that he calls flight.

"Do you think they'll like me?" Chewie asks, smacking me again with his tail. "Do you think I'll get my own pet? Do you think …?"

I miss the questions Chewie is trying to ask me because I'm sure that's Pal now. I start running, rudely leaving the pup behind, passing Wheels and then Diana and then Spike.

Pal's circling in and out of my sight, in and out of the trees on that side of the bridge. I want to call out to him, but I'm breathless, running. Pal is alive. I didn't know until this moment how sure I was that I had lost him. That the zombies had somehow won and taken another member of my family.

"You see him too?" Diana asks, catching up to me. Then we're both sprinting to the rope bridge.

It's a bit of a climb up the hill above the river, but we're excited now, and we screech to a halt next to the wooden posts the humans have hammered into the ground on this end of the bridge. The ropes are tied to wooden slats that run from here all the way to the other side of the bridge, and the whole thing sways in the wind.

"There!" Diana says as the small brown blur darts between the trees again. "Pal!"

But he doesn't answer, and he doesn't turn our way.

"Pal!" I yell as loudly as I can, throwing in one of my patented battle trills. He's going to be so excited to see me. I get ready to catch him when he makes one of his failed landings, planting my hind paws solidly in the dirt for stability.

"Is he in trouble?" Spike asks me, landing with a last bounce beside us. I just shake my head. He doesn't look like he's dodging a predator. He looks like he's weaving in and out of the trees for fun.

"What's the big hurry?" Wheels says, finally heaving himself up to where we sit, closely followed by Chewie, who pants on the ground beside us.

"The sooner we get across, the sooner we can ask him who he's playing with," Diana says, her grin slowly fading, "So ... I guess this is goodbye then, Emmy?"

I open my mouth in surprise and then close it with a click.

"Right, Emmy's not coming back to camp," Spike says, giving me a sharp salute that would delight Wally. "Honor and glory, right, Emmy?"

"Honor and ... glory," I manage to choke out.

"I don't understand ...," Chewie starts to say, but is interrupted mid-question by Wheels.

"We'll let everyone know about your mission," the

weasel promises, "starting with your friend Pal — there he is again. I wonder if he's playing with another bird?"

"Unless you've changed your mind?" Diana asks, the hope in her voice painful to recognize. "We can cross and talk to Pal together?"

They look at me expectantly, and I realize this is the moment I have been looking forward to. It is. Right?

I shake my head. That rope bridge leads back to The Menagerie. Sure, I've admitted that I was wrong about Wheels, but I declared that I was done with the camp. I am on a mission to rid the world of zombies. To go back would be to make myself a liar, or worse, a coward. How would I ever live it down?

Diana's and Spike's ears droop at my response, but they nod at each other like they were anticipating it. Chewie still looks totally confused.

"I'll go first," Spike says, stepping out and onto the bridge. She hops across carefully all the way to the end and then doubles back. "It's fine. Just be careful to step on the wood and not between. Come on, Wheels."

The weasel gingerly grabs on to the rope that serves as a handrail, his eyes locked on the wooden slats as he moves slowly toward Spike, the sharpened stick clamped in his jaw. He's slow, but Spike encourages him and guides him all the way to the other side.

"Do you see Pal?" Diana calls across, asking the question I've been dying to ask.

Wheels sits down on the other side, shaking, as Spike bounces into the woods a bit and then comes back. "No, I don't see an owl. He might have headed back to the camp."

I wish he hadn't. I wish he were on that side of the rope bridge, waiting. That makes no sense, Emmy! You're not making any sense!

Diana sets off next, placing one paw at a time on the slats. We all hold our breaths because we know her weight will put the most strain on the rope bridge. I'm gripping the wooden post so tightly that I will surely have slivers in my paws when I let go. Wheels and Spike are waving their arms encouragingly from their end, but we needn't have worried. The humans who built this were much larger than Diana, and she makes it across to hug Wheels on the other side.

"Come on, Chewie, just like I did," Diana calls.

Chewie turns wide eyes my way, and I force an encouraging nod.

"I wish …," he starts to say, and then he just gives me a big lick of affection that knocks me onto my rump. It reminds me of Ralph so much that I just sit there, unmoving. Ralph would return from his daily walks and search all over the house to give me a big lick in greeting. Sometimes we'd make it a game of hide and go lick. He found it hilarious. I wonder if I could teach Chewie to play.

Chewie turns to follow Diana's instructions, and Spike comes onto the bridge again, guiding him the way she did Wheels. Chewie's gaining confidence with every step he takes, and though he gives us a couple of scares as he wobbles, he makes it across to cheers and hugs on the other side. Chewie gives me a sad "woof" of good-bye and then follows Wheels into the trees that will lead back to the camp and The Menagerie. Spike gives me a spirited wave and bounces after them. Diana sniffs the air and calls, "Zombies to the north of us I think, Emmy. Good hunting."

And then she's gone too.

And I'm alone on one side of a rope bridge.

Perfect.

CHAPTER TWELVE

It's nightfall before I leave my side of the bridge.

At first, I'm just waiting to see that no one rushes back because of zombies or a camp that's overrun. Spike may stay to fight, but I know Diana will race back to get my help.

Then, I wait for Pal or Wally or Pickles to come back to the bridge to coax me home. I work out all my arguments while I'm waiting. They're simple but steeped in the abiding duty I feel to exterminate zombies. If they really want me to, I could go back with them to make sure everyone is safe. Just to check in, of course.

But no one comes.

In the growing darkness, I think I can see the dim glow of the humans' camp through the trees across the rope bridge. I imagine Trip's tearful joy at seeing Diana again. And how excited Connor and the rest of the human children will be to meet Spike, Wheels, and Chewie. I wonder if Pickles and Hannah will help get them set up in The Menagerie, or if they will be interrupted by Ginger and his long-winded tours that include everything that has happened at the camp since we arrived.

No one is coming.

I turn away from the rope bridge and head into the edge of the forest to contemplate my new solo mission in silence. And it *is* silent. Spookily so.

I'm in what used to be another human park, with more wooden benches and garbage bins positioned around the edges of the green space.

I climb into a small burrow at the base of a tree and sniff it. Whoever lived here abandoned it long ago. It is cold and unwelcoming. I pull some leaves and moss from the forest floor and pad it into the sides. It feels huge, this burrow. There's so much empty space.

I can't get comfortable. I scramble out and gather more leaves and moss and shove them in.

I find a few soft pine cones and shred them. I drag in some matted fur a hooved animal shed from their winter coat. A bit more dirt. Some of the pine needles that blanket this forest. I climb into the garbage bin to drag out some crumpled-up newspaper. I'm out of breath by the time I crawl back into a much snugger version of this burrow. There's barely enough room for me to turn around now, but it's better.

The bit of matted fur underneath me tickles my nose,

reminding me of Trip's habit of pulling on his own tail in his sleep. Sometimes he'll release paw-fuls of fur from his tail into The Menagerie, making Wally and the 4077th kittens sneeze convulsively in their sleep.

Has the world always been this silent? Even the crickets and cicadas are absent from the night song tonight.

I got used to Pal's deep sleep hoots, which seemed to emanate from his talons all the way up through his small body. I got to know the cycle of cat purrs that would start loud as they got comfortable in their sleeping spots and then diminish to the lightest hum as their sleep deepened. I wonder what they are doing tonight. I could drop by and check. It's not like I need an invitation back to The Menagerie, right? It's my home too.

I WAKE UP TO the sound of birds and insects. Extricating myself from this burrow is an effort, but I manage it. As soon as I'm free, I dart out through the park at my usual accelerated speed. Collecting fallen berries and other edibles as I go, I count mammals and birds, cataloguing them. I run further, faster, away from the rope bridge. I imagine my red cape billowing behind me. I listen for the sounds of zombies. Actually, let's be honest, I'm listening for the sounds of animals running from zombies.

In The Menagerie, I would split my non-zombie-killing time between the perch where Pal slept and the rooftop from which I could guard against invaders. As a nocturnal mammal, when I was sleeping, other mammals were coming and going from The Menagerie. I modified my sleep schedule because I had no choice — daytime was a constant buzz of activity and sounds. Kind of like this. But this feels apart from me. I'm not included in the work those two chipmunks are doing to fix a rotten piece of their burrow's wall. Those four mice are arguing about some seeds they've found, but they haven't seen me yet. An acorn lands on the ground in front of me, calling my attention to a squirrel with a scraggly black tail. He runs down the trunk of the tree, grabs the acorn in his mouth, and sprints up another tree, all without a word or a glance at me. I might as well be invisible.

There's something else about this quiet park lit by rays of sunshine through the canopy of trees. I slow down and close my eyes. This could be the ValHamster of my dreams. Where they say dead warriors live forever.

No more meetings. No more compromise. No more purring and hooting and giggling and gossiping. No more surprising Trip. No more impressing Diana or Hannah. No more training younger mammals in the art of warfare. No more any of that.

I open my eyes. I remember the bench with the small bronze plaque: "Being deeply loved by someone gives you strength, while loving someone deeply gives you courage." Somehow those words make more sense to me now.

I have been loved. Many times, it seems. By many animals. Mostly dogs. I loved deeply once. Did it give me courage? As well as pain? Could that be where my courage comes from? Is that what gave Wheels the courage to help me rescue Diana and Spike?

I sit down right where I am, allowing the world to buzz around me. For the first time, I think all the way through this dream of a glorious death. I will fight zombies until I can fight no more, and I will fall in battle. I know it. And then what? ValHamster, with its fields of fallen warriors. What about my friends? Will Ralph and Vance even be there? Or do dogs go to their own version of ValHamster? What if I'm working so hard to be a lone hero with no love in my life only to be rewarded with an eternity of being alone? What if *this* is ValHamster? This world where I am a hero who saves everyone?

"Help!" squeaks a terrified little voice, jarring me from my conflicted thoughts.

The source of the terror is readily apparent: the top half of a zombie is dragging its way toward a tiny squirrel on the ground. She must have fallen out of her nest in the tree above, because before the fog of war drops over me completely, I see two larger squirrels scampering down the tree trunk, cursing at the zombie with their small fists raised.

"Get back!" hisses a tiny white kitten as it charges toward the zombie from the other end of the grove. It has a very angry face for a kitten, emphasized by the single brown stripe of fur between its eyebrows. Wait, I know that kitten.

"No!" yells Sonar, running after the smaller kitten. Sonar is followed by another five tiny felines. The whole 4077th is here!

I don't have time to think about where they came from. I leap onto the zombie's back and run up to its ear, grabbing it with both paws to turn it away from the squirrel and the kittens. The ear comes off in my paws with a gross *schloop* sound, but it's enough to get the zombie's attention. That's new. Zombies are dead, so of course they're falling apart, but this one is falling apart faster than my usual encounters. Its grasping hands turn from dragging itself through the soft forest floor toward me, but I'm not on its shoulder anymore. The zombie has trouble turning (it is half a zombie, after all, and without legs, all motion is confined to its arms) but finally gets me in its sights again. It's frothing at the mouth like a rabid animal. Also new. This zombie is extra weird in a world that is already extra enough.

I wave my paws at Sonar, who has landed on the white kitten, flattening him with her weight. The rest of the 4077th follow her lead, and now there is a cat pile holding down a hissing white kitten. My blood is rushing through my veins as I consider my options at lightning speed. Can't light the zombie on fire — no matches. No big rocks to shove it onto. No wires to pull on and cause a decapitation. I'm going to have to start with that log over there.

"Come on, zombie," I hiss, letting out a loud trill and backing up slowly enough so that it thinks it can catch me. I wind up and kick the air in the kata that I learned from Spike, landing in a perfect superhero crouch Spiderman would be proud of.

Over the zombie's shoulder, I see one of the larger squirrels scoop the baby off the forest floor and scamper back up the tree trunk. I can't see the kittens anymore, but I hope Sonar has managed to order them all to safety.

The zombie, attracted by my exertions, extends an arm my way, and I dive into the hollow log. Now is the moment of truth. Will the zombie follow?

The zombie slams itself against the log. Once, twice, three times it slams into the log, making my teeth chatter like a guinea pig. The zombie falls onto its side gracelessly to glare at me in the hollow, extending an arm into the log as far as it can. I will it to try harder, glaring challenges at it from the hollow. Not glares filled with scimitars this time but carefully aimed poisoned arrows, daring the zombie to try to squeeze in here. Once the arm is good and stuck, I'm going to climb a tree and drop the heaviest branch I can right on his head, crushing him. The arm grasps at air an inch from my nose.

Grasps again. And then is still. As is the rest of the zombie.

What is going on? He's not stuck, he's just stopped moving. Zombies don't give up this easily.

I slowly climb out of the hollow log from the other side, ready to leap into battle again at the first sign of movement. But the zombie is still. The froth around its mouth is leaking out and pooling under its undead head.

I pick up a stick and poke it in the eyeball.

No reaction.

This zombie is dead, and its head is still attached.

But then how did I kill it?

CHAPTER THIRTEEN

I don't trust that this zombie is actually *dead* dead, so I keep poking it with the stick from different angles. I growl at it. Trill at it. Finally, I climb onto its back and jump up and down on it like the trampoline that was in the backyard of my first house. Sonar and the 4077th re-emerge from their hiding spot to stare up at me.

"What are you doing?" demands the white kitten with the angry face. His fur is stuck full of forest bits from his squashing at the paws of his troop.

"Starbuck," Sonar says, shaking her head with exasperation. "Emmy kills zombies all the time. Stop asking impertinent questions and get back in formation."

Starbuck will not make it far in the military, I can already tell, the way the attitude is flying off his tail and whiskers. He's more of a berserker than a soldier who follows orders — a young mammal I think I could hone into a terrifying warrior like myself. The rest of the 4077th are having trouble staying in line as well, but they seem united in their disapproval of Starbuck.

"Thank the Sabre-toothed Tiger we found you, Emmy," Sonar says, turning her attention back to me, her black tail flicking her happiness.

"What are you doing so far from camp?" I ask, wondering if my own happiness at seeing them can be read by these kittens. I've never lived with other hamsters, but Ginger and Pickles were the best at interspecies communication out of all the cats, and they said they could tell my mood by the vibrations of my whiskers. Sonar has been getting better at interpreting non-feline messages with the amount of time she has been spending with raccoons and beavers.

"We escaped," Sonar says, her tail halting its happy movements mid switch. "The humans are never sure how many of us there are in the 4077th, and we don't have pets yet, so I don't know that they've noticed yet. And Wally … that is … the General, he caused a distraction that allowed us to get away."

"Pickles told us to come find you," Starbuck announces, daring the ire of his troop by interjecting.

"All we knew was that you were across a rope bridge," Sonar continues, ignoring the younger kitten. "Diana told us where to cross the bridge —"

"Wait, you escaped from the humans?" I repeat back at them, sure I am missing something. "Our human pets?"

The kittens all nod in unison.

"But, I saw Pal …," I say, pointing toward the rope bridge.

The 4077th kittens suddenly look terrified, except for Starbuck, who starts hissing at the empty sky above us.

"When?" demands Sonar, her voice going high as her eyes scan the skies.

"Yesterday," I answer, watching as their backs slowly un-arch themselves.

"Oh, good," Sonar says, relaxing. "Raja, it's time for field rations. Take the troop in a small circle around this grove. Bring enough back for Emmy too."

Raja, a small gray cat who looks like a miniature Wally down to the Sia-like bangs, gives a quick salute and then pushes the rest of the kittens toward the perimeter with his nose. Starbuck looks like he wants to stay, but he also looks affronted that he was not chosen to lead the food-finding mission. I've also gotten better at deciphering cats' feelings from their whiskers and tails. For example, Sonar's whiskers are telling me that she's worried.

"Spill," I say as soon as the other kittens are out of earshot.

"Rabies," she answers with a shudder. "Our human pets put everyone into cages apart from each other. Pickles did her best to explain that none of us were in-fected, but Connor couldn't convince his mother."

I glance down at the zombie I'm still standing on, and the froth around his mouth.

"But Diana made it back," I say. "She told you where to find me."

"Diana and the new dog, I think his name is Chewie?" she asks, waiting for my impatient nod before continuing. "They're in their own cage, I'm not sure where. Wheels and Spike are in their own cage outside, we passed them as we ran out. All the cats are in one cage in The Menagerie. Trip was out with the other raccoons when the lockdown started, so I don't know where he is."

"What about Pallas?" I demand, scared I already know the answer from the earlier reaction of the kittens.

"The humans think Pal has the rabies," Sonar says, frowning as she passes on this bad news, "but Ginger says birds can't catch rabies, so no one knows what to think."

"The rabies came from somewhere, though," I say, almost to myself. "The humans wouldn't be isolating us unless they had proof that someone had rabies."

"An otter," Sonar confirms. "She wandered into the camp's outer fences, frothing at the mouth and shaking so hard she could barely walk. We were still trying to figure out where you all had disappeared to and what had happened around the tents when she showed up."

"Pal flew out to check on her, didn't he?" I ask, knowing my empathetic friend would be the first on the scene.

Sonar nods. "He was already looking for you and

Diana, but he swooped in and crash-landed on the otter's back. She fell over. And then he was talking to her when the humans came out to investigate. He flew off, we thought to keep looking for you, and then we didn't see him again for a day or so. The humans were rounding up all the animals in the meantime, and when we saw him, it was far away, deep in the forest. He seemed confused and kept bumping into trees."

"More confused than usual, that is," mutters Starbuck as the kittens of the 4077th rejoin us beside the zombie.

"Which is why the humans think Pal has rabies," I conclude.

Sonar nods, waiting for the kittens to pass around equal amounts of food before starting on her small pile.

"The otter, she had a bite?" I ask, taking a few overly ripe cherries offered by the kittens and popping them into my mouth automatically.

The kittens nod at me, mouths full of cherries and bugs. The redness of the cherries around his mouth gives a white cat like Starbuck an especially scary expression.

"A big bite or a small one?" I ask, spitting out a pit over my shoulder and watching the younger kitten mimic me.

Sonar frowns. "I'm not sure. Why, Emmy?"

I tap my hind paw on the zombie I'm standing on. "This zombie is dead, but he shouldn't be. We barely fought. I think he has rabies. I think maybe he bit the rabid otter, and it killed him too."

CHAPTER FOURTEEN

We're back at the rope bridge before the sun has started its descent.

"All of you?" I say again to the 4077th troop.

"All of us or none of us," Sonar says without missing a beat, reminding me of our adventure across the beaver dam when we saved Trip, Ginger, and Diana. She may have matured, but her stubbornness grew right along with her. And maybe she passed it on, because the kittens respond again with a united nod.

I don't argue with her. These kittens are not the best fighters, but leaving them out here by themselves doesn't seem like a much safer option. Worst-case scenario: I get them back to our compound, they are tossed in a cage with Pickles and the rest of the cats, and I free them all later. Even that would be a learning experience for this troop, with a low risk of injury.

I will not be captured. I guarantee that.

"We free our friends, we find Pallas, and we tell the cats about the rabid zombie," I say, leading the way toward the camp, my eyes on the skies just in case Pal flies by and we can reverse our plans. Truth be told, I wanted to focus on finding Pal because I think Ginger is right. I've never heard of a bird with rabies. Even as a housebound hamster, I knew of rabies. You caught it by being bit by another animal with rabies. And humans could be infected too. The dogs would talk about it all the time because they got annual vaccinations against it at the vet. They learned from other animals at the vet that once you are bit, rabies progresses quickly, but it can be cured in its early stages. It was obviously too late for that otter, but if Pal had somehow contracted it, I would not let the humans hurt him. I'd make them save him.

"There," Starbuck says, hissing at the orange sky.

The rest of the kittens drop into a formation Wally calls "the turtle." It is the blur of a bird, but it's not Pal. Its wings are far too wide, and it's flying very high.

"Not Pallas," I announce, allowing my claws to relax but glaring up at the not-owl in warning. If my eyes were weapons, they'd be red lasers of warning to stay away. There are other threats in this world, especially if you're traveling with six small mammals that can be carried off by large winged beasts.

Not on my watch.

The rain starts as we walk into view of the camp, plinking on the forest floor around us. Sonar is leading the troop, and I'm just bringing up the rear. The truth is, these kittens can't seem to maintain a consistent pace, so circling them meant I was bonking into them every few passes. No matter. Traveling with animals you trust makes this a reasonable approach. Plus, protecting these kittens makes me feel larger than life — like my best warrior self.

The camp looks different to my eyes, more fortified for sure, with double the number of sharpened logs pointed out toward the forest. There are more human patrols too, walking along the upper battlements. It looks more like the fortified bush of thorns the wigs/guinea pigs lived in. I don't like it. It's odd not to see Ginger or Diana patrolling with them. The tented area where Wheels' pet turned into a zombie and attacked us has been burned to ash. In fact, it looks like many things have been burned in this spot, zombies and animals alike.

"The cats are being kept in The Menagerie," Sonar reminds me, "but the pets blocked off Pal's perch, so the only way in now is the main door from the human sleeping quarters."

I would prefer fighting my way into The Menagerie, but these humans are not our enemies, and I don't want to damage our camp with fire. Plus, the rain would make fire a difficult weapon to wield. That leaves one-to-one stealth combat. A silent fight that doesn't attract the attention of a mob. Something these kittens are not good at.

"We need a distraction, Sergeant," I say to Sonar, "preferably on the other end of the camp. You take care of that. I will free the animals."

Sonar nods immediately and starts sending off signals through her whiskers and tail. Starbuck's whiskers clearly transmit back some cuss words he should not know at so young an age.

"Starbuck, we need a signal who can keep an eye on everyone," Sonar says, pointing at the tree above us. "Emmy needs you to get up as high as you can. We all meet back here when our missions are successful."

I nod at her proposed strategy. She has absorbed a lot from Wally and I, and she's passing it on like a leader should. When we're all back together in The Menagerie, I'm going to ask her to recruit Chewie into the 4077th troop. He would benefit from both the camaraderie and the confidence being part of a team instills. The way these cats did for me.

Meanwhile, Starbuck isn't sure whether he should be flattered at being singled out or annoyed that he's being left behind, but he gives Sonar a minimal salute and starts scrambling up the tree. I give him a boost, and he pulls himself up by the claws, getting up about five feet before looking back down with a grin of triumph.

"Good hunting, Emmy," Sonar says, and then leads her troop off to the opposite end of the compound through the trees.

"Good hunting, Sergeant," I repeat back at her.

I feel the cloak of war drop over my shoulders, but it's with a calmness I'm not used to. I pick out the first human I will need to evade. She's one of the tallest in our compound. One of Hannah's pets, I believe. She is hanging over the edge of the barricade, her arms folded over the wooden logs that serve as a handrail. I slide through the pointed logs and run up one, silent as the night. I wait until Hannah's pet takes a moment to wipe the rain from her eyes, and then I squeeze between her feet. Deftly, I tie her shoelaces together where she stands. She gives a tremendous sigh, and I freeze, heart pounding. When she doesn't scoop me from between her feet, I hazard a look up and see that she's just resettled her position over the handrail. Perfect. Trip taught me how to tie knots using his favorite sparkly shoelace, and I think this one would make him proud.

I look for my next target. Those two men will do. One is wearing bright red pants, and the other has a moustache as big as me. A crack of lighting lights the sky momentarily, and then I'm off, dashing between barrels and boxes and ropes. The two men are ten feet in front of me. Six. Two. I screech to a halt behind them as they turn.

"Did you hear something?" the older one asks, scratching at his hamster-sized moustache.

They glance back at where Hannah's pet still stands staring out over the battlements.

"Nah, just the weath … whoa!" yelps the other one as I scamper up the inside of his right pant leg.

"What?" I hear the older one demand as the owner of the pant leg starts smacking at his legs in a panic. I head for his hip and, spying a hole in his pocket, wiggle my head through. His frantic smacks make contact with my back end, and I rip through his pants and land on a box beside him wearing the red cloth of his pocket around my neck.

The men are arguing about what just happened when we all hear Hannah's pet hit the ground with a curse. I leap down to the wooden floor, the red pocket cloth flapping behind me, and sprint to the door to the pets' sleeping quarters. Nothing can stop me now. I'm through the doorway and in complete darkness when I hit something soft and low to the ground. I rebound with a growl, rolling to the nearest wall to refocus on my adversary.

"Emmy, shhhh!" says Connor's voice. Before I can do any more than lower my claws, he sweeps me up in his sticky fingers and shoves me unceremoniously into the front pocket of his overalls. I don't fight him. Out of all the pets I have met in my lifetime, I trust young Connor the most. He would never betray us. I know that in my bones.

"Connor, what are you doing up?" says a sleepy adult voice.

"Pickles," Connor says in answer, "want Pickles."

"Pickles is fine, you can see her in the morning," says the adult voice, scooping both of us up, Connor and his stowaway hamster.

Connor takes a deep breath that I know foreshadows a level-three hissy fit, and I clap my paws to my ears. Obviously the adult knows what is about to happen too because they immediately say, "Okay, okay, we'll peek in on Pickles. Really quick. And then right back to bed."

"Pickles," crows Connor, releasing his breath and patting his front pocket a little too excitedly.

This wasn't how I'd planned to gain access to the cats, but it gets me through a closed door, so it works for me.

"There, see, the cats are fine," the adult voice whispers, walking through the humans' sleeping area and opening the door to look into The Menagerie. I can hear the cats meowing, but I don't dare stick my head out of the pocket so close to an adult in this brightly lit room.

"Pickles, Wally," Connor says, straining against our captor, his hands reaching out.

"Tomorrow," the adult says. "Connor, stop playing with the light switch."

"One, two, three," Connor says, flicking the light off.

"One, two, three," I repeat under my breath, under-standing immediately what Pickles' young pet is telling me.

"Good counting," the adult says to Connor with a quiet laugh, flicking the light back on.

"One, two, three," Connor says, flicking the light off and grabbing me out of his pocket. I leap out of his hands, hit the floor at a roll, and hide behind one of Trip's small blankets.

"Enough," the adult says, flicking the lights back on, "but good counting. I have to tell your mom ..."

I lose track of what the adult is saying because they start to pull the door closed behind them. I peek out from under the blanket to see Connor waving at me with a smile from over the adult's shoulder before the door is shut. Smart kid. As loyal as one of our dogs. His love for Pickles and the rest of us gives him strength above and beyond his years.

I step out from under Trip's blanket to face the shocked faces of the cats in the cage and allow myself a huge grin, paws on hips, wearing the red pocket cloth like the cape I have earned.

CHAPTER FIFTEEN

"Tell me again," Wally says as I wrestle with the pin holding the cage door closed. My paws aren't as dexterous as Trip's, so this is my third attempt.

"The 4077th is causing a distraction," I repeat, grunting, "on the opposite end of the compound so that we can get out."

"You left them on their own?" Hannah asks. I'm standing on her head because she's the tallest cat in the cage.

"The sergeant has been well trained," I say, daring Wally to disagree.

"Harrumph," is his only spoken answer, though his tail is expressing his wish to disagree.

"Sonar's got this," Ginger says, leaning his full weight against the cage door so that when I do get the pin free, he's the first to tumble out. Thankfully, this cat has the grace of four felines, and he rolls into a pirouette that looks choreographed.

"You seem different, Emmy," Hannah says to me as she helps me climb back down.

"I am," I reply. I mean it. I feel different. And it's not just the cape.

"She's talking more, that's for sure," Ginger says. "I like it."

"So, what's the plan?" Pickles asks Wally.

Wally nods at me. "We need to get everyone free to regroup and convince the humans that this new cage policy is unnecessary and insulting. Emmy and I can free the dogs if you three can find the rabbit and the weasel."

"How about I go with Emmy to free Spike and the weasel?" Ginger proposes.

"Wheels," I correct automatically.

"Right, Wheels," Ginger says. "You're the only one they've actually gotten to know. They might trust you rather than some random cats they met just before being captured. Plus, we still don't know where Pal or Trip are. We don't want misunderstandings to slow us down." He's on the balls of his paws when he says this, which means there's something important in his words.

"This isn't a misunderstanding," Wally blusters. "The owl is a danger to all of us. Humans and animals alike."

"Wally," Pickles starts to say as Ginger's back literally starts to arch in front of us, the orange hairs standing on end.

"I've got one of these boards loose if someone could

stop arguing and help me," Hannah says, pushing a board out of the way of Pal's usual exit from The Menagerie with her paw and head.

"Fine," Wally snaps, shoving us all up the ramp that leads to Pal's perch. "I don't care who rescues whom, just get everyone out that you can."

"We meet at the first tree of Trip's tree-to-tree highway, where Starbuck is waiting for us," I say. "He's the white kitten with the angry face."

Wally looks incredulous at this latest reveal of strategy involving the 4077th, but before he can do more than gape at me, Pickles pushes him out onto the perch and calls over her shoulder, "Good luck."

"Good hunting," I answer.

WE DIVIDE AS SOON as we're out in the wet night air. The rain has doubled in its ferocity, and the cats go from determined to miserable immediately. I've never seen weather take the wind out of a mammal's sails like rain does to felines. Wally looks at my red cape like he'd like to use it as an umbrella, and I stare back at him, daring him to try.

"Come on," I say to Ginger, who is grimacing up at the rain like he can guilt it into stopping. He shakes his fur and each of his paws before he follows me out onto the battlements, where we carefully make our way around to where the outdoor human litter box sits. We keep expecting to run into one of Ginger's pets, but whatever distraction Sonar has put into action seems to have worked. We can hear human voices on her end of the compound, but they don't sound panicked to my ears (which would have roused the other sleeping humans).

"Why are we going for Spike and Wheels rather than Wally?" I demand as soon as I can no longer see the other cats.

Ginger shakes his fur again. "Really? Now?"

"Now," I say, crossing my forearms and waiting.

"Hamsters," Ginger says, looking up at the rain again as if that will make me give up. I don't care. It can rain till Ragnarök as far as I'm concerned.

Ginger comes to that understanding quickly. "Fine, like you heard, Wally's not exactly open-minded about the whole Pal-rabies situation, and Pickles is on the fence. Hannah says we're overthinking it all, and Diana is such a peacemaker I don't know where she will land. I want less debate and more action, which I knew you'd be into. Plus, I figure you've got pull with the newbies seeing as you saved them and got them back here in one piece."

He's right. I know I have created valuable new allies in Wheels and Spike. Usually it's the cats or the raccoon who bring in new mammals, but this time, it's all me and Diana.

"And I *know* birds can't get rabies," Ginger says, flicking his tail at the rain. "My pet before all this was a doctor, and we watched a lot of looooong medical documentaries. Trust me. We need to be the ones to find Pal and figure out what's going on with him."

I take off, because that response not only makes sense but lines up with my plan perfectly. We need to find Pal. ASAP.

A black and silver goat sits behind the shed-like structure, chewing on a piece of hay, completely oblivious to the ruckus and the rain.

"Hey, Jammies," Ginger calls down to the goat. The goat glances up at us and then returns to her way more interesting meal of tin cans and hay.

"Jammies, get yourself together, this is an escape," I hiss down at the bovid.

"Escape? From what?" Jammies answers, not even looking up at me.

"You're tied to the humans' litter box," Ginger reminds her.

"I chewed through that rope weeks ago, see? Tasted like hard spaghetti. In a good way. Anyway, this is where I like to be," Jammies says with a snort. "Not all of us have a fancy manger built for us."

That stymies us for a second until she says, "This is the best spot in the camp. This big box here? It's filled with human food scraps. Your fat racoon wishes he lived this close to garbage nirvana. Ask him. He tries to get in here at least twice a night."

"You could share," Ginger starts to say.

"You could go fall off a log," Jammies replies.

"Wow," Ginger says, "and you wonder why no one wants to hang out with you."

"No, I don't," Jammies says.

"Never mind," I growl at both of them, "do you know where the rabbit and weasel are?"

"Weasel?" the goat repeats, actually stopping her chewing for a moment. "Weasels are the worst. They're worse than cats. They're worse than dogs. They're worse than —"

"We get it!" Ginger says. "You don't like anyone. Super clear. Have you seen them?"

"Maybe I have, maybe I haven't," the goat says, returning to her maddening masticating.

"That's it," I announce and throw myself onto the goat's back. She immediately tries to buck me off, arching and kicking her single powerful hind leg in the air. But I'm not that easy to shake. I've ridden zombies into battle. And bears. And ravens. This goat has met her match, and it's a mad hamster named Emmy.

"Where are they?" Ginger demands as he leaps down into the muddy ground, nimbly dodging Jammies' flying hooves.

"Show us," I loudly advise the goat, who is still trying her best to shake me loose. "The sooner we get the weasel and the rabbit, the sooner I leave you to your precious box of garbage."

"Get off me!"

"Nope," I reply, and I hang on even tighter as we dance around the orange cat like the world's worst ballroom dancers. Jammies throws herself into the garbage bin, and I'm covered in detritus and smelly things, but I hold on. Breathing is for lesser mammals. I am a warrior. And I have friends to save.

"Argh!" Jammies whinnies, abruptly stopping her bucking. "I was wrong. *Hamsters* are the worst."

"Truer words have never been spoken," I say agreeably. "Now take us to Spike and Wheels."

Jammies gives one more shake to make sure I won't be dislodged and then takes off at a run with Ginger following us. She leaps over some barrels, and my cape flaps behind me as we are airborne. I have a moment to wonder if any other hamster has spent as much time in the air as I have before she skids to a stop at the opposite corner of the yard from The Menagerie.

"The cage was on that barrel when I —"

"Help!" Wheels calls from somewhere out of my sight.

The goat saunters to the other side of the barrel, where we see the cage.

It's sinking into the mud because of the hard rain.

"Emmy," Wheels says from inside the cage. "You found us."

I scamper straight off the goat's back onto the cage, running all over it, looking for the cage door.

Ginger slides into the mud, trying to get his shoulder under the cage. He may be the vainest cat I know, but when it comes to his friends, he will do anything for them. Including covering himself in wet dirt of questionable origins.

"Can you get it open?" Ginger calls up, his white paws sinking into the mud with the cage.

"The cage door is underneath us," Spike says weakly, blood around her left ear. "We were trying to get out, and the cage fell off that barrel onto this side."

"Spike is hurt," Wheels says, pulling at the rabbit's paw, trying to drag her out of the sucking muck. He's got one paw wrapped around the top of the cage and one paw pulling Spike up.

"The goat's horns," groans Ginger from under us.

"What?" I say, reaching between the bars and grabbing Spike's uninjured ear, pulling with all my might. She squeaks in pain, the clearest indication that yes, she is hurt. Hurt enough to not be able to hide it. Wheels lets go of the cage and wiggles down to get under her, pushing her up on his shoulders.

"Jammies," Ginger yells. "Pull this cage out with your horns."

The goat has been watching all of this with limited interest and says, "Why would I do that?"

"Because someday you might need our help," I growl at the selfish bovid. I've got a good grip on Spike now thanks to the weasel's boost, but Wheels' lower body has disappeared into the mud. He's holding the rabbit above him with a strength he should not have. His arms are shaking, but his face is determined. I wiggle out of the cape with my free paw and shake it down through the bars at Wheels.

"Get Spike out, Emmy," he says, locking eyes with me and grabbing one end of the long red cloth in his teeth.

"We're getting you both out," I reply, holding tight to Spike's ear with my right paw and to the cape that is keeping Wheels above the mud with my left. I will not let go. I will never let go. I have the strength of ten hamsters. It will be enough.

I turn to yell at the goat again, but she's no longer there.

Ginger slips in the mire and drags himself back out with effort, his claws marking deep grooves in the dirt that get filled in with mud almost immediately by the rain. He spits dirt and yells up at us, "Jammies took off. Hold on, I'll get help. We can't do this on our own."

I nod through gritted teeth, I've got Spike, and she's holding on to the top of the bars with her paw, but though I'm still holding tight to the red cape, I can't see Wheels at all anymore. I tug on the red cape, and I feel tension on the other side. He's still holding on. Damn this rain!

"Och! Hold on, lassie!" says a hedgehog's accented voice somewhere above us. In a tree, I see Trip and Malone and Starbuck all staring down at me, along with three other raccoons I don't recognize. Trip is already digging in his fanny pack, and he pulls out his long, sparkly shoelace that we practice knots on.

"Hold on, Spike, Trip is here," I whisper down at her, my own arms shaking now as well from the strain of holding on.

She blinks up at me through the rain. "ValHamster?"

I shake my head with effort. No way. Not now.

"We live. We are loved. We are strong because of it. We *live*," I say through gritted teeth.

Trip leans out of the tree holding one end of the shoelace, and Malone throws himself down holding on to the other end. The hedgehog has to tie the shoelace to the cage because I have no free paws. Spike's fading out of consciousness, her ear going limp in my paw.

Malone ties the shoelace and tugs on it to give Trip the go-ahead, and the raccoons start pulling from their position in the tree above us. The mud makes a greedy slurping sound as we move upwards, as if it doesn't want to give up what the rain has gifted it.

"We've got you, lassie," Malone says through the bars of the cage, reaching through and trying to grab Spike too, but his arms are too short.

"Malone, the weasel," I say to the hedgehog beside me. "He's under Spike in the mud somewhere on the other end of this red cloth. I can't reach him ... He's ..."

"I see him, lassie," Malone says close to my ear. "I see him."

And as we are pulled free of the mud by the strength of the racoons, I see him too, lying at the bottom of the cage, coated in mud so thick he looks more like an otter than a weasel. He's curled in a ball, still clutching his end of the once-red cape.

Ginger finally returns, followed by two of his humans, and meows up at the cage now suspended half a foot above the mud by a sparkly shoelace.

The humans share a shocked look and then set to getting the animals out. They take the two limp bodies in their arms and run for the shelter of the medical room. I am collapsed on the top of the cage, the rain battering my face as I struggle to regain my breath. With Malone's help, I climb down off the cage and follow Ginger and the humans.

"Wally said that weasel was better at playin' dead than even you," Malone says, pushing me along in the rain, "and that bunny's as tough as a pub fight after a lacrosse game. Don't you worry. We'll get them fixed right up."

I don't answer, barely managing to put one paw in front of the other, my muscles in full rebellion. I don't even flinch when Trip scoops me up in his paws, carrying me and Malone the rest of the way under his arms like two footballs.

Trip puts me down gently at the back of the room. We all watch the humans race around with medicines and bandages and water.

"We left them out there in that cage. We did this," the shorter one says.

"The bunny will make it," the other one says, though she sounds worried. "She got knocked around when the cage fell, but I think she's just concussed. I'm going to clean her head wound."

Trip is up on the counter, stroking his tail rhythmically. "Spike is moving," he calls down to the rest of us on the floor. "She's blinking a little bit. Coughing too."

"See, lassie, I toldja," Malone says, poking me with his shoulder quills. I barely feel them.

Ginger, who looks like an entirely different cat covered in mud, calls up to the raccoon on the counter. "What about Wheels?"

Trip looks back down at us, tears flowing from his masked eyes.

"I can't," says the shorter human. He raises his eyes

from the table where he's been working on Wheels to the woman who is now gently washing out Spike's wounds with water. "He's … gone."

The woman's eyes widen, and she scoots around the table to examine Wheels herself.

"No, let me," she says, leaning over the weasel. "No, no, no."

The man looks at Trip on the countertop and then down at all of us gathered on the floor of the medical room. "We're so sorry."

Spike reaches for Wheels from her table with shaking paws.

I calmly climb up the cabinet and onto the counter. The humans seem to understand why I'm up here and back away from Wheels, turning to focus on Spike, whispering to each other. I kneel at his side, press my ear to his thin chest. We are both good at playing dead after all. I listen. For a sign. For a beat. For a breath. I wait. But in my warrior's heart I know. He has earned his place in ValHamster.

CHAPTER SIXTEEN

We send the weasel on to ValHamster in the red pocket cloth I tried to save him with. The cats want to wrap him in it, but I am determined that he wear it as a cape for his fiery journey. He will wear it and walk amongst the honored dead with pride. Ralph and Vance will welcome him, I am sure. We set him afloat on the river we crossed together in a small wooden boat carved by Spike's teeth and Trip's engineering skills. We stand on the shore and watch the flaming vessel until we can see it no more.

The humans of our camp are distraught that they caused the death of an innocent animal, something Connor makes sure they take responsibility for between crying, clutching Pickles to his chest, and then angrily kicking at the cage that has been relegated to the corner of The Menagerie. I understand how he feels. It's exactly the reaction I had when I lost Ralph and Vance to our pets. So much anger. So much blame.

Connor is ramping up to a new record: a level-five fit, according to the rapid-fire whisker signals flying between Wally and Pickles. Pickles is having trouble breathing, her pet is holding her so tight. I step forward to pull on the young human's pant leg, and he looks down. I raise my paws to him, and he picks me up. Everyone in the room is silent, watching us. I run up his chubby arm to his neck and nuzzle him like I've seen the cats do count-less times. He finally releases Pickles from his grip, and she drops to the ground, sending signals of thanks back up to me through the flicking of her tail. I can be his strength in his despair. The way these cats were in mine.

Chewie howls in commiseration but is settled by Diana and Trip on either side of him. He's been hard to con-sole since he heard about Wheels, flinching at every loud noise, doubting his place amongst these humans. Once Connor and Chewie settle down, the human adults clear The Menagerie, discreetly picking up the discarded cage, leaving us alone.

Connor's mom gives me a nod of thanks and then scoops her still sniffling child up. I land back on the floor with a thud, and Spike leans on me because she's still not back to full strength. I'm proud of her because she's not trying to look tough.

The humans have gone out of their way to restore the coziness of The Menagerie after the cage fiasco. The blankets are newly washed, the litters are pristine, and the fire pit has new glowing stones giving off a pleasant heat. There's also a fresh bowl of food for each of us that none of us are eating (though I notice Trip keeps glancing at his to make sure it's still there).

The cats gather around the pit. Diana takes a seat too, and Chewie follows her as he has been basically since he got out of that guinea pig hole. Spike and I stand at the periphery, she because she's never been part of our sit-down talks and me because usually I'm orbiting the group rather than sitting amongst them. I decide it's time for that to change.

I help Spike to sit next to Diana, who shifts over with a surprised smile. I take a seat between Diana and Chewie.

"Well, let's hope that never comes up again," Wally says, giving his bronze star a rub. "If we locked up all the healthy humans because of the zombies, I wonder how they would take it? A bit of an overreaction, to say the least."

"You mean like you did when Pal went missing?" Ginger throws in.

The room goes silent at Ginger's words. I feel the urge to start orbiting again, but then Chewie lays his tail in my lap. He's falling asleep for the first time since this ordeal began for him, and I'm not going to be the one to disturb his feelings of safety.

"They panicked," Trip says, wrapping his own tail around himself. "I've panicked lots of times. It's kind of my thing. Though my panic doesn't usually result in locking up my friends in cages."

"Are you saying I panicked?" Wally demands of the animals in the room.

Spike, Ginger, and I nod in unison, earning a scowl from the older gray cat.

"All we're saying is that before Malone and Sonar get back with the 4077th, we should probably have a plan for next steps," Pickles says, her hesitation vibrating off her whiskers. "For Pal, I mean."

"I'll say it again: Pal is not sick, at least not with rabies," Ginger says, crossing his paws under his orange body. "We need to find him, for sure, but not because he's a danger to us."

"He probably needs our help," Hannah puts in. "If he's not sick, and not looking for Emmy, then he would come home."

We all contemplate the owl out in the world on his own. It's not a fate I would wish on myself anymore, and definitely not on my best friend.

"Look, I can admit when I'm wrong," Wally starts to say.

"You haven't," I interrupt.

There's another pregnant pause as the mammals look from Wally to me and back again.

Wally swallows. "I was wrong. I reacted like my human pets. I escalated us to DEFCON 1 without any real proof that Pal had rabies. That was a mistake."

"Yeah, it was," Ginger says, earning a rolled-eye response from half the room.

"We all make mistakes," I say in response, surprising everyone. "I made a mistake with … Wheels. And with all of you. I kept you at tail's length.

"I pushed you away." I direct these words specifically at Diana. "I was scared to feel again. To love again. To speak again. To give voice to my pain. After Vance. After Ralph."

I look at Spike. "But being around Wheels taught me that my courage comes from love. And that your love makes me strong. I'm far stronger than any hamster before me. That must be because I am more loved than any hamster before me."

I swallow hard, suddenly thirstier than I've ever been in my life because this is the longest speech I've ever made. But warriors are brave, even in the face of scary truths.

Ginger whistles through his teeth. "What the Sabre happened to you all out there?"

"Well, I killed a zombie without taking his head,"

I reply, remembering the other important thing I learned when I was alone.

"You did what now?"

"I think he bit the rabid otter," I say, nodding to myself. "Before we find Pal, you should know about that. Just in case. Might be important."

"Rabid otter …?"

"Emmy can kill zombies without decapitating them now?"

"Forget that, Emmy loves us!"

"I knew she loved us, but she said it! Out loud!"

"What *did* happen out there?!"

"Hold up, hold up," Diana says, holding up a paw for emphasis. "Emmy, what are you talking about? With the zombie, I mean. Start at the beginning."

So, I describe it all. The baby squirrel falling out of the tree, the sudden appearance of Starbuck and Sonar and the 4077th, and the zombie, lying prostrate at my paws after a minimal battle.

Wally strokes his star as he thinks. "Not to jump to conclusions (again), but what you're saying is that zombies can be killed with the rabies virus?"

I shrug, ready to move on to finding Pal now. "I'm just telling you what I saw. The zombie had the froth around the mouth. And I heard the otter had a human mouth-sized bite on her. You can ask Sonar. She saw too."

"We're not doubting you, Emmy," Diana says. "We're just wondering if there's a connection between the rabies and the zombie you killed."

"The zombie who died," I clarify. "To be honest, I don't think I killed him at all. I think he would have died even if I wasn't there."

"And now she's not taking credit for a zombie kill," Ginger murmurs under his breath. "The world has turned upside down. Again."

Trip waves the orange cat's wonder away with his black paws. "Okay, okay, so you remember those humans who were experimenting on raccoons at that other camp?"

We all nod. It's a story he's told a few times since his triumphant rescue of almost two hundred of his kind.

"They were testing something on the racoons," he says, pulling at his whiskers as he remembers. "They were doing it with a needle. Injecting the racoons with something they thought would make them not turn into zombies even if they got bit."

"You're saying this could be what the humans were looking for?" Hannah says, eyes wide. "A cure for zombies?"

"Wait, wait," Wally says, shaking his bangs at us. "We're not going to be able to persuade the humans to get infected with rabies to test if that will save them from becoming zombies."

"Connor is convincing when he's mad," Pickles says, "but I don't think even he could explain this to the adults."

Wally and Ginger step forward, and now all the cats are debating about the rabies and how to explain this to the humans. Whiskers are vibrating, tails are flicking back and forth at different speeds, it's a full-on feline feud.

"We're going to find Pal, Emmy, don't worry," Diana says, sidling up next to me.

"But this could be the difference between a zombie-filled world and going back to normal," Spike says from my other side. "This is really important too."

Hard to disagree with that logic. Plus, up until now, defeating the zombies meant finding each one and destroying it. That could take more than one hamster's lifetime. But if we could make it so the humans were vaccinated and no new zombies could be created, that would make eradicating the whole zombie population within my grasp.

"You knew I'd come home on my own," I say to Diana. "That's why you left me out there alone. You knew it wasn't for me, this whole master plan I had of a solo mission with no family and no one to fight for."

Diana's tail end starts wagging in a way that I know means she's pleased. She's basically nodding with her butt.

"You told Spike and Wheels," I say, waiting for Spike

to verify my suspicions with a nod before asking, "But what would you have done if I hadn't come back?"

"There was no chance of that," Diana replies with confidence. "You said it yourself. Not even the greatest zombie killer in the world can live without love."

"But what if —"

Diana is already shaking her head. "Then I would have found you out there in the wild. I would have brought everyone, and we would all have joined your solo mission until you were ready to come home."

"If it's your mission, it's our mission," Spike says.

"That's what family means," Trip says from his food bowl, where he has finally given in to his cravings.

Their words create a warm feeling in my being. A much stronger feeling than the sadness. Even stronger than the anger.

"The cats will figure out how to pass this information about rabies and zombies on to the pets," I say, looking around at my allies. "Meanwhile, we will find Pal and bring him home."

"You mean split up?" Diana asks, looking back at the sleeping puppy with worry in her eyes. "Isn't that the opposite of what we've been trying to do? We were trying to get back here. Back to these mammals."

"You were right; we'll always have them. This is our herd," I say looking at the circle of felines with love and feeling my courage rise. "We have two vital and glorious missions before us: one for the cats and one for us. Pal is out there by himself. We will bring him home."

I DREAM OF A glorious life.

I am a warrior, and every day is filled with friends and family to protect.

Who needs a cape?

ACKNOWLEDGEMENTS

Winning the Hackmatack award for the first book in a series you're writing is a pretty awesome event, so I have to start by thanking all the fans who have read, and wrote in and supported Pickles and her fellowship of zombie-fighting animals.

My husband and daughter spent a whole pandemic lockdown listening to me talk about *ValHamster*, so I must thank them as always for their love, support, and patience.

Big thank you to my team at DCB: Barry Jowett, my editor, the fabulous Sarah(s) and Chantelle. You are wonderful and brilliant and I have so appreciated your support and ideas throughout this process, especially while we've been socially isolating.

Lauren at the Owl Research Institute, thank you for answering all my crazy questions about Pallas and burrowing owls in Canada. I promise, I will include more of your answers in book 4.

To the teachers and librarians who continue to bring Pickles and Portia into their classrooms and introduce them to generations of young readers, thank you, you've created lifelong readers and fans.

To the indie bookstores like BookCity on St. Clair W, Queen Books on Queen East, Another Story in Roncy and the Mysterious Bookshop in NYC, who continue to carry my books and speak of my characters to your readership, thank you!

Big thanks to Shelagh Rogers and Marc Côté for your faith and continued support.

Thank you to the Ontario Arts Council for supporting my work.

And finally, I must dedicate this book to Champlain, the latest cat to sidle his way into my heart (you might recognize some of his personality traits in Sonar), and my very own Pickles who is putting up with Champlain's antics as best she can.

Angela Misri is an author and journalist of Indian descent. She was born in London, U.K. and briefly lived in Buenos Aires be-fore moving to Canada in 1982.  Angela is the author of the Tails from the Apocalypse books, which began with the Hackmatack Award-winning *Pickles vs. the Zombies* and continued with *Trip of the Dead*. Her other work includes Portia Adams Adventures series and several essays on Sherlock Holmes. She earned her BA in English Literature from the University of Calgary and her MA in Journalism from the University of Western Ontario. As a former CBC Radio digital manager and the Digital Director at *The Walrus*, Angela is never offline (although she prefers to write long form in notebooks). Angela plays MMORPGs, speaks several web languages, and owns too many comic books. She currently lives in Toronto.

Photo by Eugene Choi

We acknowledge the sacred land on which Cormorant Books operates. It has been a site of human activity for 15,000 years. This land is the territory of the Huron-Wendat and Petun First Nations, the Seneca, and most recently, the Mississaugas of the Credit River. The territory was the subject of the Dish With One Spoon Wampum Belt Covenant, an agreement between the Iroquois Confederacy and Confederacy of the Ojibway and allied nations to peaceably share and steward the resources around the Great Lakes. Today, the meeting place of Toronto is still home to many Indigenous people from across Turtle Island. We are grateful to have the opportunity to work in the community, on this territory.

We are also mindful of broken covenants and the need to strive to make right with all our relations.